Randy: The Full and Complete Unedited Biography and Memoir of the Amazing Life and Times of Randy S.

Mike Sacks

T0026710

CONTENTS

INTRODUCTION

In the spring of 2019, while visiting my family in suburban Maryland, I stopped at a garage sale, in Poolesville, about thirty miles west of Washington, D.C.

At these sales, I tend to pore over LPs, books, old postcards, and any other interesting gimcrack or geegaw that catches me ol' fancy.

I'll typically purchase at least one item. An old VHS tape. A "Best Of" LP from a 1970s rocker that I could always hear on the radio for free, if I ever had an inclination to do so, which I typically don't. A clock shaped like a Maryland crab. A "gently worn" Baltimore Orioles T-shirt. *Anything. Just one damn thing. Don't be rude, Mike. Buy something!*

So, at this particular sale, I bought something. Specifically: a book.

It was at the bottom of a large cardboard box, beneath a dozen or so moldering issues of *National Geographic* and *Smithsonian Magazine*, two essential publications in any D.C.-area home.

I flipped through it.

It felt a bit *off*.

Way off.

Awful.

Was this an elaborate joke? An art school project? What in the hell *was* this, exactly? A work of genius by a writer with Nabokovian pretensions? A work of garbage by a writer with Nabokovian pretensions? I was confused. How did the owner first come across it?

I asked. He didn't remember. Neither did his two teenage children. *Maybe from a library book sale? Or from the spring flea market at church?* Shrugs.

The manuscript resembled any "book" that an author could zip off at a Kinko's or create by slipping an endless stream of quarters into the copying machine at a public library. The spiral binding was of the cheap plastic variety, the kind used for company employee manuals or the menus at 24-hour Greek diners.

On the cover was a simple layout—*very* simple—with the following somewhat lengthy title:

Randy!
The Full and Complete Unedited Biography and Memoir
of the Amazing Life and Times of Randy S.!
Written and Typed by Noah B.

Beneath the title was a photograph of a young-ish man whom I assumed had to be this "Randy." He looked to be standing on a street within some type of suburban development. It wasn't clear whether he was trying to appear tough or heroic or intelligent or bored or excited—he was just a guy standing on a suburban street.

I thought: *So who the fuck is this Randy S.? Is he well known in the D.C. area? A politician? A famous lobbyist? A local celebrity of some sort? And who exactly is Noah B., the writer and typist of this book?*

The original price was $9.99 but it was being resold at the garage sale for twenty-five cents. I paid with one dollar and told the now former owner to keep the change. I'm generous like that.

Back at my parents' house, in my old childhood bedroom, in which to stay can be a surreal experience in the best of circumstances, downright hallucinatory at others, I read the book in full. When I finished (after two, three hours at the most), I immediately returned to the very beginning—and began again.

I had never read anything quite like this work of … *what*?

It was a biography of a local thirty-something named Randy S. and it took place over the course of roughly a year and a half, from August 2017 to February 2019.

Randy worked at various retail gigs and odd occupations before he came into money. He liked women a whole lot. He had, let's just say, pedestrian tastes when it came to TV shows and books and music.

Randy had many ideas for creative projects that he hoped to one day get off the ground. For instance, he had an idea for a "clean yet efficient" device to kill insects. The invention would be called an "Insuck-Ta-Side," a vacuum-type appliance used for sucking up bugs. The insects could then be humanely discharged back into the wild. Simple. Safe. "Girls will love it."

Another idea: flavored sex lubricant. Suggested flavors would include barbecue, peppermint, hot spice, Tropical Breeze, and Chocolatini.

This way, women, too, "can enjoy the process."

Randy's favorite method of relaxing was to sit in his big fluffy recliner and just "chill," usually in front of his flat-screen television. The recliner had five pockets for remotes. Also, a cup holder big enough for a Big Gulp.

And a vibrating foot massage.

Randy was a self-described "outside the box" thinker. He loved hitting Ocean City, Maryland, on summer weekends but not in the winter when there was more "riff raff." His favorite Baldwin was William because he wasn't as "puffy" as the rest of those "jokers." He didn't like the Beatles but he did adore Aerosmith (but only the *mid*-career years), as well as the 1980s supergroup Asia.

In Randy's opinion, the U2 musical *Spider-Man: Turn Off the Dark* was "unbelievably underrated." So was the little-known Huey Lewis and the News' 2001 album *Plan B*.

As were "clean and odorless" women.

As were "deaf women."

So there was that. But was there anything else to Randy? Had he accomplished anything of any worth?

Not really.

But … well, here's one thing:

Randy's grandmother, whom he called his "Mam-Mam," died five years before this book was originally self-published in April 2019. Mam-Mam was not a rich woman but she did own a considerable plot of land outside D.C., with a non-working farm and a 19th century house in which generations were raised, including Mam-Mam and Randy. The entirety of Mam-Mam's will was left to Randy after she died of a heart attack in February 2014, including the large plot of land that Randy promptly sold to a suburban developer for a tidy sum ("more than six figures, less than seven, but still enough to strut").

So what did Randy do with this newfound windfall? Did he purchase a new home instead of living in Mam-Mam's? Well, yes. He purchased a brand-new, $1.5 million, six-bedroom town home that sat atop the hill overlooking his former farm, which no longer contained Mam-Mam's old house. It had been torn down.

Did Randy purchase a new car to replace his 1989 Pontiac Grand Am? Why, yes. A "gently used" 2010 Hummer H3 with vanity plates that read "RNDY84".

Randy's most important decision—at least as far as we're concerned—was hiring a writer (the aforementioned Noah B.) to move into his brand-new town home to live with him for eighteen months in order to pen his life story. While Randy is a "brilliant" writer, he has dyslexia and words tend to get all "a-scrumbled." Also, he never "quite learned to type" and he wasn't about to start now.

Noah, the author and typist of this book, was a recent graduate of the University of Maryland, with a degree in literature. Struggling to make it as a poet and fiction writer after moving back home, he noticed an ad Randy had placed on Craigslist.

Noah applied for this interesting—if somewhat unorthodox—gig, got it, and then proceeded to move into Randy's town home to live with his new arts patron in order to capture the genius of Randy on the page.

Beats working in the retail world, right?

I was taken aback by it all. The book I had stumbled upon was a modern-day version of a 15th century biography commissioned by a wealthy Medici patron, flattering and complimentary and prone to purple prose, but with more references to flat-screen televisions and the Bloomin' Onions at the Gaithersburg, Maryland Outback.

This book that you now hold in your hands is an honest and fascinating (and very suburban) take on a very individual character. If this memoir were to somehow wind up buried and discovered centuries from now—perhaps beneath Randy's extensive Aerosmith CD collection—a future reader could seemingly do a whole lot worse than to dip into this skewed, steaming slice of 21st century American political, social and pop-cultural gumbo. (That is, of course, if a future reader would be able to understand Randy's very unique 20th century coinages for women's anatomy.)

Although Randy's online thumbprint isn't huge—just a simple website, as well as Twitter and Facebook pages—I did manage to locate him within a few days. It wasn't the toughest of assignments: Randy was still living in the same town home that's described within.

Randy was very happy with me reaching out. Confused but thrilled: *How did you find the book? Only three hundred copies were printed! Why do you want to re-publish it? Will all proceeds go to me? Will I now become famous?*

So much for my original theory that this book was a work of Nabokovian pretensions. There was no irony intended with this book.

Yes, I assured Randy: beyond the printing costs, all proceeds would, indeed, revert back to him. I had found the book at a garage sale in Poolesville. I didn't know how the owners had found his book or why they'd ever want to part with it. I wanted to re-publish his biography and have more readers discover it. I found it fascinating and thought that others would also. I wasn't making fun of it. I truly found it incredible. Offensive at times, but incredible.

On the other hand, no, Randy would most likely *not* become famous. Sorry about that. Or maybe he would. Who knows?

Negotiations lasted just a few days. Our only major disagreement seemed to hinge on whether or not to publish last names (including Randy's), as well as the photographs included in the book. He very much encouraged me to do so. He wanted to get "laid." Why else would he and Noah spend more than a year writing a book? "C'mon, dude! Please! I *mean* it!" Randy was only half kidding. Or maybe more than half. It was difficult to tell.

We came to an agreement. Last names wouldn't be used. We live in a litigious culture. *Something* in this book was bound to offend *someone*, especially those who reside in either the same development as Randy or live in the same town. I'm a freelance writer. I can barely stay afloat when all is going well, let alone when defending myself (or Randy) from incoming and ongoing litigation.

But here was my concession: if Randy wanted to announce his own last name in the press *after* the book was published, that would entirely be up to him.

As for Noah—whom I talked with for three hours over the course of a few calls—he's still pursuing his dream of becoming a published fiction writer and poet. He's still living with Randy. "It's a comfortable situation, one that I'm not entirely happy with, but it'll have to do, at least for the moment. No one's hiring writers. And my dream book—a novel about a twenty-something American living in Madrid who's going through a spiritual crisis—doesn't look as if it's going to be finished any time soon! I have to visit Spain first! As for *this* book, my job was to chronicle Randy's life. That's what I signed on for. That's what I was paid for. To be his loyal retainer. I really hope I did him justice. And I will say this about him: He's a *captivating* piece of work!"

So here's the book.

Would I want to ever hang out with Randy? Truthfully, no.

But to read about him from a good, safe distance, well … there are worse activities.

I'm confident and hopeful that there will be future Randy biographies down the road. He's still so young, only in his thirties! He and Noah could pop out additional volumes every few years—and could do so easily! It would be the modern-day equivalent of the diaries of Samuel Pepys … if Pepys partied his ass off at Club Seacrets in Ocean City, Maryland.

Another note: I have not changed one word from the original version, beyond abbreviating last names.

As they say, "it is what it is."

I hope you enjoy.

Mike Sacks

Chapter One:
THRILLING BEGINNINGS!

Randy S._____ steps from out of his town home and onto the second-floor balcony overlooking I-270. The morning traffic heading east from Frederick into Washington is moving steadily but slowly.

Randy takes a sip from his favorite "LET'S DO THIS!" mug, filled with steaming instant coffee, with just a hint of Vanilla Yoohoo. This man is thirty-four years old but looks no older than twenty-five. He is especially well endowed with an imposing physical brawn as well as a once-in-a-century intellect. His voice is most pleasant to find oneself listening to: melodious. Harmonious. Agreeable.

"I hate a few things in life," Randy says, carefully stepping around his above-ground jacuzzi. "Not many. But a few. Guy librarians. Homeless people with attitude. Movies that end with a twist. Black and white movies. Obviously, *The Wizard of Oz* sucks. I just have no patience for it. I hate the manager at the Baskin-Robbins on Rockville Pike. I despise him. He minimizes the number of pink-spoon samples I'm allowed to take. For him it's five. I need at least 10. But this was before they delivered, so that changed some things."

Randy pauses. And then continues in his deep, plummy voice:

"Time to backtrack. My Mam-Mam raised me. My father is dead. Everyone hated my dad. That's what people say. Supposedly he had tattoos on his balls. One read 'Salt,' the other 'Pepper.' He died onstage at the Frederick Bluegrass Fest, karaoking 'Kokomo'. He was jammed up off the reds. It wasn't even his turn to sing. With two you get egg roll, right? Cry me a sad one.

"As far as my mother, she ran off to breed another family in California when I was twelve. She saw the movie *Hair* on Cinemax and got the hippy dippy dreams in her spacy racy head. She met a deaf plumber, Chuck, who owned a motorcycle. I met him once. Chuck gave me a high-five. He taught me how to deaf-sign to Bon Jovi's 'Livin' On a Prayer.' I still remember. A good bar trick.

"My mother's life was always a rollercoaster. Some real loopy-di-loops. Some real intense twists and turns. Sometimes I refer to her as *Gland*-y. Her woman glands always seem to be in overdrive. Her real name is Gladys. She's a dizzy, daffy dame. *All aboard the S.S. Female! Looks to be choppy waters ahead!* Best of luck to her. Has she written her autobiography at the age of thirty-four? I think not. But the world can thank her for giving birth to the Dandy Randy!"

Randy sighs and spits between his bottom teeth in a masculine, enchanting manner. He lights up a Backwoods Wild n' Mild, tapping the ash out over his balcony's railing. "I don't know where I get my smarts, my genius." He puffs handsomely. "In some ways, I'm just like everyone else, normal. In other ways, I'm not. A *serious* dichotomy!"

Randy takes another glance at the cars on their way to work on I-270 and blows out a beautiful stream of honey-flavored cigar smoke.

"You know," he says casually, "after I die, which I can't see happening for a super fucking long time, but when I do die, I'd only want to be remembered for giving great hugs. Also, for being incredibly rich and having a gigantic fucking cock."

Randy impishly winks.

"Sure the recorder is on? Good. A little closer please. I want to accomplish *so* many things over this next year, but I want to accomplish two in particular. One: I want to be the very best neighborhood association president in the history of Maryland, but most especially here in Fernwood Pines where I reside. Wait till you see how I operate! It's like the pool scene in *Boogie Nights*. *Everyone* loves me. And I love them back!"

The morning traffic heading east from Frederick, Maryland into

Washington D.C. has slowed to a crawl.

"Best neighborhood on earth. Two: I want to find my inner amazing. I want to dig down deeper than I've ever gone before. I want to spelunk into my inner soul. Bore into my own damn self. I want to explode and burst into flames of ideas and *awesomeness*."

Randy flicks what's left of the Wild n' Mild onto the ground below.

"Give you some history. *All* heroes have history. My Papa died when I was ten and I remember him for a few reasons. Here's one:

"Have you ever heard the saying, 'Life is a water flume. There are ups, there are downs, you get splashed and you get wet but then you towel off and climb back up the stairs to do it over again and then you get wet again'?

"I've heard it, I don't remember where it's from. Ben Franklin? *The Last Airbender?* I can't remember. It's a beautiful quote. I've always liked it very much and found it to be more than true—almost *very, very* true.

"I've always loved Jolly's Waterpark in Ocean City. My favorite Jolly's attraction was the giant wave pool. It's like being in the ocean but without all the piss and shit. If there is piss and shit, the chlorine will take care of that.

"I'm in the pool. I'm around nine. On a raft. Back then, you were allowed to bring a blow-up raft into the pool. Before the Rules Committee took over the country. I'm floating and dropping, floating and dropping, just bambling the fake waves. I'm staring at the sky. I liked to look at the clouds and imagine each of them as human body parts. I *still* do that. Like that cloud resembles a breast. *That* one is an elbow. Maybe a fibula. *That* one looks exactly like the webby toes on a freak. Things like that. It's fun.

"I'm looking and dreaming when, out of nowhere, I find myself in the water. This isn't good. Mam-Mam never paid for swimming lessons. She thought I could figure it out for myself like she had at Ol Man Rymer's Swimming Hole. Ol Man Rymer was a sick fuck and his left eye was all hibbly jibbly, but he had a great hole for swimming. People say it was the best hole for swimming. And they're saying this even though a lot of kids drowned. That's an *awesome* hole.

"Back at Jolly's, I fall off the raft. I lose consciousness. I'm *out.*

"I find myself floating through a long tunnel. Not a water tunnel. An *air* tunnel. It feels like I'm experiencing a giant O, which I don't feel in real life for another two years. That's when I climb and hang on to the twizzly rope in gym class. Peppery yum yum. It's like that in the pool. Everything feels bingo gango. I feel warm. It's like I just drank a tall glass of orange juice after being crazy thirsty. I'm being sucked into this long tunnel and I don't mind. People I don't even recognize are lining the sides. Maybe they're dead? They're telling me that it's all okay: *Do not stop. Just keep flying down that tunnel toward the light!*

"I see the woman who played 'Hot Lips' on *M*A*S*H.* She's standing to the side. Not in the shitty movie but from the awesome TV show on channel 5 repeats. I've always had a crush on her. I can also see the mother from *Who's the Boss,* with the eyebrows that are brown and the head of hair that's blonde, which I love, because you never know what color surprise you'll find down below. It's like a carnival game.

"Then I see my PopPop. I haven't seen him for so so *so* long. He's off to the side. He's just as I remember him. He has a very kind look on his face. He says, 'Randy, keep going. It's *okay.* I'll be there waiting for you.' But he doesn't say this with his mouth. He says this with his mind. It's *incredible*!

"I feel encouraged that he's telling me to move forward. If he's saying it, then it must be okay. I won't get hurt. PopPop is watching over me.

"I do as he says. But man, something just isn't right. See, PopPop isn't dead. He wouldn't die for another six years. He's still fucking alive. So what's he doing in the magical tunnel? Why is he telling me to go forward? Is he a dick? He left Mam-Mam because he thought she was old and ugly. But would he really encourage me to walk towards my own death? What an *asshole*!

"Next thing I know I'm being kissed by a teenage dude by the side of the pool. On hot concrete. I'm no longer in the tunnel. He's blowing into my mouth, his breath all stinking of Cheetos. Now, in typical circumstances, like when watching TV or watching the neighborhood moron, Mitch, scream at insects, I absolutely *love* Cheetos. It's the perfect food to eat when watching something cool take place. Not now.

"Standing next to this dude lifeguard is a beautiful girl lifeguard. Any reason *she* couldn't have given me CPR? It had to be this ass? The guy goes to touch my stomach but before he does, I roll over and barf out wave-pool water. The crowd is grossed out. Some applaud. I'm not sure what the girl lifeguard does. Maybe she feel sorry for me, which isn't always a bad thing."

Randy lights up a fresh Wild n' Mild. This one, Russian Cream flavored.

"*Whammo!* I punch the dude lifeguard in the dazzlers. Someone says, *'That guy just saved your life!'* The lifeguard scrunches over and falls to the ground. The female lifeguard *tsks-tsks* that way hot lifeguards do. I leave quickly. Even then, at nine, there's a mystery about me. I come and go as I please. I'm a phantom. I play it all cool. Mam-Mam picks me up outside the entrance but she's late, so I have to wait. That's uncomfortable. I see a lot of people who've just witnessed me nearly drown. Some even imitate me barfing. The dude lifeguard limps past. He looks at me like, *Why did I just save your life?!* Whatever. Is he writing a memoir at the age of thirty-four? Didn't think so."

Randy floats out a Russian Cream O-shaped ring.

"My brain changed after that, you see. It was rewired. My brain exploded into a million and trillion fragments. I became a superhero. I began to think differently. I began to pulsate with differentness.

That's lasted to this very day. It ain't always easy, but it's always fun. At least for me!"

Randy spits again between his bottom teeth. It's a move similar to any that could be seen in the world's most popular American action movies.

"So *that's* a good story. I got a ton of 'em. The straight life ain't for me. Hail no. I've always wanted *more* out of life, especially after dying. For me to be happy, my legacy needs to *last*. This is vital! I want my legacy to even outlast the great Dandy Randy!"

He points to himself. His meaning is clear.

"PopPop's side wanted to turn this place, this subdivision, into a park. A *playground*. They claimed that there was this *special* spider. It was protected. That, *even if I wanted to,* I couldn't sell the farm! Because this *special* spider lived right here on the land. I took care of *that* special problem!"

Randy motions as if shooting down a row of spiders with a machine gun.

"Wah *wah*! Bang *bang*! Bye *bye*!"

Randy puts down the imaginary machine gun and waves hello to a neighbor. No one can resist a friendly wave from Randy!

"That's Mrs. T._____. I know everyone who lives in this development. *Der commandant.* One of my rules here is that everyone has to hang a funny flag. Mine is a crab wearing a University of Maryland Terps hat. Mrs. T.____ has the O's bird giving the finger. I love it all!

"I come up with all the rules. No one else. Everybody loves the meetings. We eat, drink, gab. It's my favorite night. We're *family*."

Miss Y._____, an attractive middle-aged woman out walking her chocolate Labradoodle, calls up to Randy: "Randy, we have to talk about the winter fund for the leaf blowing and snow shoveling."

"That can wait, darlin'," says Randy. "We have months and months. But first we have to talk about the funny mailboxes! Gonna be *mandatory*!"

"*Darlin'*?" asks Miss Y. _____. "Well, okay then."

"She's real nice," says Randy, as Miss Y. _____. walks away. "But not as playful as I like from my kittens. I like 'em real *rambunctious*. She couldn't make it to the last association meeting. 'Had to work.' I know that's not true. I can't tell you how I know but I do fucking *know*.

"As for Mam-Mam, everyone knew she was dying. I hired a hospice nurse to make her last days as comfortable as possible. I couldn't afford to hire a real nurse. What to do? I hired one in front of the Highs where the day workers congregate. A very nice Mexican named Valentina. I think she's Mexican. I never asked. Actually, her name might not have been Valentina.

"I gave her an incentive: 'The longer Mam-Mam lives,' and I said this real slow, real drawn out, 'the more money you're gonna make.' Her eyes lit up. By the end, she was making $11 an hour. That's great!

"Mam-Mam eventually died and I wanted to ask for my money back but you can't do that. It's the only profession with a zero percent success rate. Pathetic. Anyway, Valentina wasn't medically trained but she made *amazing* Hispanic rice and chicken. A rose con popo, or something."

Randy blows a thin one to the heavens above. Takes another puff. And then another for good luck and because it looks cool.

"We almost hooked up," he continues. "She'd wear this crisp white nurse outfit, and whenever she'd clean up Mam-Mam's spittle or doody, I would kind of catch her looking over at me.

"It's funny. Mam-Mam just kept getting more and more woofy. Sick with the goofy goof. She would call me 'Jimmy' and her cat 'Sponge.' Never even owned a cat. She started screaming out the wrong answers to *Wheel of Fortune* ... but truthfully she did all this before. She began to water her plastic plants. Gave her dentures a bath in Sprite. Sip her coconut prayer oil. She refused to eat the popcorn we loved, sprinkled with Old Bay. I've always despised old people!

Not Mam-Mam but the rest. Too many 'what's'? That smell of cheap talc. Their pea-soupy breath. Their powdered-milky eyes. They smell like medicated powder and sadness and they're always offering you crappy hard candy. And they're a lot closer to death than your friends. It's like watching someone race a marathon in a wheelchair. They're gonna finish the race first, they're definitely gonna win. But so what? Is that an *accomplishment*? Meanwhile, it's annoying and tedious to watch!

"You can see it in their eyes. I once ran over an old woodchuck with my three-wheeler with balloon tires. Used to ride beneath the powerlines. I ran over him and I stopped and I looked down. And he looked up. And I swear this is true, he mouthed, '*Why*?' But looking into his eyes, it was like looking straight into death. And that's what I'm talking about with old people. They can *see* it. And *you* can see it in *their* eyes. Not fun!

"Anyway, Valentina insisted on reading biblical verses to Mam-Mam, which pissed me off. So I forced her to read Dean Koontz. Out loud. The last thing Mam-Mam ever heard was the beginning to *Demon Seed*, but half in Spanish, which might have confused her. There are worse things to hear when dying. Especially if you have the 'heimers. It's my all-time favorite book!"

A young woman, down below, walks towards her parked car. She is Natalie D._____ and Randy calls over, "You coming to the next meeting? Gonna be a crab boil! Right here! Classic!"

"I don't think I can make it," the woman yells back, climbing into her SUV. "But thanks anyway!"

Randy smiles. And then, softly: "She's full of shit. I know damn well she can make it. She never does anything on weekends, except watch stupid reality TV and talk on the phone with her drunk mommy. I know this for a fact. I won't tell you how. But I fucking *know*.

"Do me a kindness? You keep sticking that recorder in my face. I don't mind the attention, but just a little *farther* back? You still recording? *Hello*? Yes?"

Randy's "LET'S DO THIS!" coffee mug is now empty. He takes one last glance at the cars on their way to work on I-270. It's a steely glance that hides a million stories.

"You know, after I die, which I can't see happening for a super fucking long time, but after I do die, and it's bound to happen, if I'd want to be remembered for anything, it'd be for giving great hugs. Also, for being incredibly rich and having a gigantic fucking cock."

Randy laughs, "What!! Did I say that already? If I did, just keep it in. I want this to be an *honest* memoir."

Randy flips "the bird" to the cars—*suckers!*—and flicks the cigar stub over the balcony.

He grandly retreats back into his town home. There is a *lot* to do today.

The day is just getting started.

There are so many possibilities for Randy:

Driving to Hoops, the sports bar in the Rio mall to watch the Washington Capitals.

Driving through downtown Rockville and beeping at attractive women.

Free coffee at the tire rotation place.

Television.

But Randy has already decided on what he wants to accomplish first and foremost, and it's a good one:

"C'mon. I have to take another shit. Go grab my top hat. I want to wear it on the groaner!"

Another amazing start to another phenomenal day for Randy!
Let's do this!

RANDY-ISMS!

"Never trust a dude who points with his pinkie."

"The more talented the drummer, the less reliance on his drumstick twirling."

"If you are a retarded character in a film, you're a whole lot less annoying if you're from the South."

"Any song with a tambourine sucks."

"Mustaches only look fetching on dwarves and midgets."

"Urinating your name in the snow is acceptable. Shitting it is not."

"No good can come from hot-tubbing after the sun rises."

"Never be the one to start or finish a stadium wave."

"The fatter the friend, the more they will lecture you on dietary advice."

"Anything goes better with Old Bay. Even *that*."

"There ain't no cool way to eat a popsicle."

"Only chicks in musicals enjoy kissing in the rain."

"Only chicks in musicals enjoy talking with homeless people."

"Flavored dental floss should never be sweeter than the foods you want to get rid of."

"Flying superheroes get laid the most. Superheroes who swim, the least."

"Only assholes valet park at the mall."

"Any movie is better off with a hot-air balloon or a talking chimp."

"Always remove the bar-code from store-bought flowers."

"Never allow your fashion sense to be dictated by 'island' culture."

"The fourth season of *Crank Yankers* was the worst."

"If you bring a mitt to a baseball game, you're an idiot. Only drunks catch foul balls."

"The more *fancy* a man's signature, the more the dude is *hiding*."

"Cordless phones always disappoint eventually."

"Libraries are basically homeless shelters."

"Avoid any stripper named after a domestic car."

"Ketchup is for losers. Mustard, *winners*."

Chapter Two:
THE TRUTH!

There are quite a few urban legends surrounding Randy and his exceptional, *sui generis* life.

Here is but one: immediately after he was born, Randy took his first walking steps. Not after a few months. Or even a few days. *Immediately.* The doctors and nurses had never witnessed anything quite like this. The national press was notified. Randy became the most famous one-hour-old in the world.

This isn't true. In reality, it took Randy a mere thirteen months to get up on his feet and walk, and then even less time to start tearing his way through life.

Another urban legend involving Randy has to do with him making love to over 25,000 women. This is also not true. Randy has slept with exactly forty-six women, all carefully notated and rated in his "Fuck Journal," the lined Mead with the Yosemite Sam sticker on the cover, both guns blazing. It sits just next to his "Fart Journal."

The two journals are charmingly displayed on the Dekon 2 Tonelli glass coffee table that sits proudly in Randy's spacious living room within his $1.5 million town home.

Randy has consummated sexual relations to completion 2,457 times, in three states: Maryland, Virginia and Florida. Of these actions, he would rank 1,264 as "five," meaning the *very best.* He would rank 1,014 as a "four," meaning the second very best. And he would only rank thirteen of these 2,457 events as a "one," meaning the *very worst.* And not one of these *ones* is necessarily Randy's fault: "Mostly just girls with an inferiority complex around someone they definitely find more attractive."

Sadly, there also exist a few legends that are of the less impressive sort, specifically those that involve Randy and his various run-ins with Maryland state police departments.

Let it be known that Randy has the *greatest* respect for the police and for the dangerous work these brave civil servants perform on a daily and nightly basis. Randy imagines that it might be more than a little difficult to put your life on the line for the protection of one's community. In fact, Randy considers himself very good Facebook friends with a former police officer he's known since the fifth grade. The policeman's name is Alan P._____.

As children, Randy and Alan would light ping-pong balls on fire and watch as the orange-black flames licked the sky. Years later, long after Randy was already on his separate, successful path, Alan was arrested for lighting the woods on fire in Cabin John Park to impress a waitress at the China Gourmet Bistro in Cabin John Mall. She was not impressed. Five people died. Alan P._____ is no longer a policeman.

As for Randy's arrests ...

In a story that has been widely reported in the local press, but reported *incorrectly*, Randy was involved in a March 2009 altercation outside a senior citizen center in Rockville.

Randy patiently explains: "It was just a big mix-up. This was when I was younger and much more stupid. Only still in my twenties. I was drunk off cheap wine and had just eaten a huge meal at Bob's Big Boy. A plate of them Pappy Parker's Fried Chicken and Waffles. *Kablooey!* My stomach went off kilter. *Way* off plumb. I was on my way home but knew I'd never make it. It's like a World War II pilot who's unable to return to base safely. I don't want to sound like a hero. It's just that I was past the PNR. That means 'point of no return.' So I ditched. An elderly is looking out his window and sees me below. He was on the first floor. I was squatting like a mother. Of all the luck. He calls the cops. I was out the next day. Ironically, this asshole was a World War II vet. But he was never a pilot. You can hear this asshole's 9-1-1 call if you go onto Youtube. It's *hilarious*. He mispronounces 'defecating.' What a dick!"

Randy tells me this fascinating story while driving his 2010 Hummer H3 to Absolute Electronix on Redland Road to have a remote-start system installed. Randy despises these cold Maryland mornings.

"I love *all* types of music," declares Randy, suddenly and without prompting. "*All types of music*!!"

The rock music in the Hummer is blasting something ferocious.

"Anything *good*. I don't care what it is, as long as it's not alternative or punky or edgy or bluegrass or country or classical or reggae or any of that shit. I hate island culture. I like *melody*. Melody. *Melody!* What's so hard about melody?! My biggest musical influence is probably the 1980s super group Asia. They released only two albums but they're both *insanely* amazing. Loved Asia since I was a damned kid! Strange name—as far as I can tell, not one person in it is from China. I also love Jefferson Starship. 'We Built This City.' They built it on rock and roll. How cool is *that*? Yeah. *I like dat*!"

Randy pauses. "Listen." He flicks on his Pioneer Stage 4 DEX-P99RS, and the lush sounds of "Heat of the Moment" blasts through the $124 Alpine Direct Fit PSS-31GM speakers.

"YOU CAN HEAR THE QUALITY IN THE MELODY AND IN THE LYRICS!" Randy screams over the delightful, synthy rock. "IT'S ALL IN THERE! YOU JUST GOT TO BE LIKE AN EXCAVATOR AND HEAR IT! AND I CAN HEAR IT! I LOVE ASIA!"

The music is turned to a lower volume. Randy's voice returns to its regular, most agreeable level. "I can't scream. It ruins my vocal cords. I'm a songwriter and singer of some renown. I've written over 200 songs on Garageband. Play *all* the digital instruments. What I'm about to say is hard to talk about. But I *do* want this in the book. I have to be completely up front. People can always see through bull-shit, believe me."

He pauses. He glances out the driver's window.

What he's about to say won't be easy for him to talk about ... and yet he bravely pushes forward regardless:

"Okay. So. I *have* played ball with the law. To me, it's a game. Like a kitty cat teasing a barn critter. I admit it. I find it *fun*."

Phew. It's out there. Randy visibly breathes easier. A great weight has been lifted off his broad shoulders. "I do want to get out the *truth*. Not the crap the *Potomac Almanac* keeps reporting. That's one of the reasons for this project. Among *many*. Gonna vape now. Might want to open your window. 7-Eleven Slurpee flavor. Bingo *bango!*"

The traffic is snarled on Rockville Pike. We have at least twenty minutes until we arrive at Absolute Electronix. Randy turns off Asia and switches over to his favorite radio program, *The Sports Addicts*, on 106.7 FM. The boys are talking in a funny manner about how the Washington Wizards never seem capable of pulling off a vital win in the playoffs: "The Wizards ain't nothin' but a batch of dribbling doofuses!" The Addicts laugh. Randy is barely listening to the hilarity taking place on the radio. He is full-on concentrating on what he's about to say. When he does finally get to it, it comes out in a beautiful torrent.

"It's June 2010. I'm working at the Pen Boutique in Montgomery Mall. I've risen to the rank of assistant manager. I sell exotic pens, desk accessories, leather business items. The job's okay. At least I'm inside, with air conditioning. Auntie Anne's is across the way, which I super, super, super love. Mini pretzel dogs. *Whoof!*"

Randy, without notice, breaks into a very funny and very loud barking spree. It lasts for more than one minute and it goes by very quickly.

"So when I'm not waiting on customers, I'm writing songs. Jotting down ideas. I have a *million* of 'em!

"I'm a brilliant writer but I did grow up with dyslexia. Words get all a-scrumbled and a-bumbled. I'll admit to that. A customer comes into the Pen Boutique one day with a sick kid. Bald head. The kid had cancer but is getting better. I'm happy to hear that. I rub his head for good luck, which he loves. His mother is buying a pen to write thank-you notes to all those who visited him in the hospital. I ask the kid about his stay. He says, 'The food sucked.' I tell him I disagree. *Vehemently*. I *love* hospital food. I eat at the Shady Grove Hospital cafeteria all the damn time! There's a ton of Jamaican cooks who make kick-ass beef patties. That's the *only* aspect of island culture I like. No one ever asks what I'm doing there. Sometimes I wear a surgical gown I bought at a used clothing store. Maybe they think I'm a world-famous surgeon? Name it and *claim* it. Blab it and *grab* it, you know?

"I say to the kid, 'Wasn't there *anything* you liked about living in the hospital? *Anything*?' He tells me that yes, there *was*. Musicians. Clowns. Jugglers. Performers who do it for *free*.

"This gives me an idea. I shoot up to the hospital with a guitar. This is the next day. The nurse at the entrance asks what I'm doing there. I tell her I'm performing for the sick kids. What I don't tell her is that I really want to do more live performing but haven't had much luck booking gigs. Talk about a receptive audience! I ask her, 'Where is the cancer for kids section?' She tells me that's it on the fourth floor, and I go on up.

"I don't wait for permission. Randy Dandy don't wait for *nothin'*. I just start strumming that guitar. Kids start gathering. Even the nurses stop to watch. I bounce into a kid's room and bang into a new song I wrote called 'Life is Funny.' It's about a mouse who lives in the pocket of a kid's T-shirt. The kid is about to die in the Holocaust. It's based on that movie about the cool dad pretending that both him and his son aren't in a concentration camp. It's all a big game. I fucking *love* that movie. I think it's the best Holocaust movie ever made!

"In my song, the kid dies. I go to another kid's room and crank out a blues song—think early George Thorogood. It's about how you can't always hook up with the hotty you think you can when you're young. *Right?* There's a lot of irony in that song. And truth. And sadness. And energy. The kid is really enjoying it! Clapping. Trying to. It's hard with the needles.

"When I get to the third room, the cops arrive. This kid's asleep anyway. See, this is what frustrates me and what the papers never get right. I was not *playing* the guitar. I was only *pretending* to. I don't know *how* to play the guitar. The guitar was the blow-up kind. Plastic. You see them at weddings and kids' parties. So that was incorrect. Also, my songs are not dirty. They are *realistic*. Sometimes *too* realistic. They are for music lovers of *all ages*. I think the kid later died."

Back in the present, Randy beeps his horn and shouts at the driver to his left to move the "fuck over."

"You know, if I had to do it all over again, I'd ask permission to sing first. Maybe play songs that weren't so bluesy or depressing. Something poppier and more upbeat. Less about death. Less about selling your soul to the devil, I guess?"

Randy lights a cigarette and rolls down his window. The traffic is particularly bad today. But this doesn't seem to affect Randy. Like most successful, affluent citizens, he has few pressing obligations.

"Okay, so when I was arrested again, in 2013, I'm no longer working at the Pen Boutique in Montgomery Mall. I was fired because I had too many suggestions. And because I was eight-balling a chick behind the knife counter. She worked at Forever 21. More like Forever *45*, if you know what I mean and you do. Then I went to work selling big screens at the Big Screen Store in Rockville. *Big-ass* TVs."

Randy taps the wheel of his Hummer. "Here's the thing about me. I hate imperfection. Physically. It depresses me. A bigger bunch of toads you'll never find than the ones I worked with at Big Screen. *Really* ugly. Like ancient hairy people you'd see living by a creek on the History channel. But there was one I got along with great. His name was Goose. *Goose*! He loved strippers! He's really the one who got me into all this here trouble. Truly! It's Goose's fault!

"See, Goose shows me a picture of an escort he knows by the name of April. Mid-twenties, nice blond hair. A substantial pair of Darwin's Dinglers. I *have* to meet her. I email her and she writes back. She seems interested but only because that's her job. It's very easy for me to tell. Some people can just 'read' other people better than others. I'm a good people 'reader.' Everyone has a 'tell.' April's particular 'tell' was that she told me she wanted to 'fuck' for 'money.'

"Fine. So I throw her a surprise. I ask her to go see a movie with me. She's definitely not expecting that one, right? She recommends *12 Years a Slave*. I say yes even though I never heard of it. She tells me what the movie's all about. I'm thinking it must have a kick-ass rap soundtrack. I love rap. My favorite rap group is 3rd Bass. Two white guys. One used a cane but he could actually walk just fine. It was just a prop! *Brilliant*. Steppin' to that A.M.!

"I was wrong about the movie. Not a second of rap. It's four hours of guys running through fields. The soundtrack sucks. I turn to April and say, 'Let's hit Dave & Buster's.' She smiles. I *have* her. The D&Bs on Colesville Road in Silver Spring is the very best. The burgers are truly legendary. All of the managers know that I don't like my buns wet. I like 'em toasted and on the side, not touching the meat or the goddamn pickle. *Full-metal burger*.

"April and I walk into D&Bs like we own the place. The manager on duty that night, Ken, nods. That's all it takes. He knows the routine. Past the bar, past the bathrooms, into the far-right corner, my chair facing out. I always like to see who's approaching me.

"I never play the video games at D&Bs, for a number of reasons. One, a lot of Chinese kids are always hogging my favorite games. Two, I hate touching the joysticks *before* I eat. Guess what? I then have to wash my hands incredibly well again. Three, I have an addictive personality. Once I start, it's pretty much impossible to stop. And I'm *competitive*! It's like my paper towel collection from rest stops. A few years ago, I took one piece home from a rest stop on my way back from King's Dominion. Then I brought home a few more. Before you know it, thousands are hanging all over my bedroom. It's the biggest collection in all of southern Maryland. They're all different. Each one. They're like the wood trolls Mam-Mam used to collect. Wood only. She hated plastic. There's one guy in Baltimore who has more paper towels but that's in fucking Baltimore."

Randy take both hands off the wheel to excitedly point at a license plate on the car ahead of his.

"Holy shit! *Holy shit!* I *love* vanity plates! I love figuring these out! I *hate* puzzles. Can't stand crossword puzzles except if it's in the *TV Guide*. But I love these … Eight! You! El. El. Love! R! *Ain't you love her!* Ain't *you* a lover! No. *Hain't* you liffer! Hmmm. *Eat you later!* Meat ain't— Eight you liff … Eight you *lose* … Eight you … Eight you *LIPSTER!* Hate you later—hate *lifting, laughter loving*, eight radar riff eight *hapes* apes are *lifting* laughs against *waiting … waiting for eight lifters …*"

Randy grows tired.

"Wait a second. I don't think that's a vanity plate."

Hands back on the wheel, he continues:

"April and I still go to the movies, every other Sunday. Sexually, April is the very, very best. She's H.A.S.B.Y. *Hot as shit in bed, yo!* Knowing her is like taking a ride down Splash Mountain but without the water and with more of the craziness. A *wily* piece of womanhood! She has no problem making her thumb go numb. Making her finger into a *stinger*! She knows what to touch and what *not* to touch. So much easier than a normal girlfriend or wife! And I can have fun with her. She lets me twist her nipples as if I'm drawing an Etch A Sketch. She knows when to talk and when to shut her yapper. She understands, at times, I can get lazy. And when that happens, she doesn't grow upset. She only knows it's time to take care of herself. A woman's privates remind me of a Shar Pei puppy. A ton of folds surrounded by a ton of fur. *Confusing.*

"Please don't even get me started on oral sex. It's like controlling a fucking helicopter. Left, *up*, right, *yaw*, lift, *drop*. But I've watched a fuck-ton of military docs. I can pull it off. It's like taking over the controls and then radioing to the tower: *Hey! I'm new here! What should I do! How do I land this contraption?!* And then you just fucking *do* it. Muggy as a jungle! *Help!*

"April also knows that I have to listen to The Sports Addicts whenever we're doing it. I like to multi-task and I think sex should be fun. I honestly believe that! I really do! If I want to chew while we screw, then I should be allowed. If I laugh out loud, that should be fun, too. Or even a chuckle. She's free to chuckle herself. I once performed oral sex on her by licking '404 ERROR RESULT.' She laughed like crazy! I'm fine with all that! Equal billing. *Feminism—*

"*Oh, look at this fucking bitch, turning without a signal!* Incredible! Hate driving on this road. Not the same as it used to be. Too many goddamn *people*. No farms anymore. Everything's built over."

Randy flips the finger to the driver in the next car but doesn't miss a beat:

"So on December 1, 2013, April and I are at D&Bs. This has all been well reported. Like I said, we saw *12 Years a Slave* and it sucked. But for some reason it gets us super bang-bang horny. Snake needs *milked*. I can't explain it."

Randy suddenly grows quiet. It's a story that has been widely reported on the local TV news, but, as is typical, it was reported *incorrectly*. It is now Randy's turn to tell the story as it *truly* happened.

Randy good-naturedly explains: "It was just a big mix-up. I was drunk off at least fifteen Razzleberry Smashtails. Maybe more. My head wasn't screwed up right. The press made it sound as if we were going at it like two feral monkeys at the zoo. *Not true.*

"But there were two problems. One, we used the handicapped stall in the women's room. Just our luck that a handicapped *woman* was at Dave & Buster's that night. How often does this happen? Fucking *never*. Handicapped *men*? Sure. All the *damn* time.

"Two, my Ipod was playing REM's 'Everybody Hurts,' which depressed the hell out of everyone in that bathroom. The handicapped chick complained the loudest. Like she doesn't have *enough* to fucking worry about!"

We're now pulling into the parking lot of Absolute Electronix on Redland Road. The lot is full but Randy manages to quickly find a space. (He always does … thanks to the very clever bootleg "handicapped" sign placed around his rearview.)

"Third, April is *that* loud. But that's her job, right? You'd think people would understand that! What's she being paid $250 an hour for? To quietly play fucking Parcheesi?!"

Randy is now exiting his Hummer, striding purposely. As he enters the store, he laughs. "She has to earn her money, right? And it's not like I pay her any *less* to sit on her fat ass through movies! Same damn fee. So she really *does* have to give it her all when we're scrumping."

And then, gently: "Anyway, it's all Goose's fault. So *that's* a good story."

"Randy!" screams an Absolute Electronix employee. He's wearing a red work vest and a nametag that reads TONY TONE. "What you here for today? Another stereo?!"

"Tony Tone! My wallet is hotter than a backyard smoker and I'm burnin' to buy!" retorts Randy.

Tony Tone laughs very, very hard. It is extremely funny. "By the way, meant to ask but couldn't at the last party: whatever happened to your midget sidekick? That black one you used to pay to follow you around? The one with the lobotomy lookin' scars?"

"He die. Car accident. Gone," says Randy, appearing sad.

"Geez. That's too bad."

"Lil Mac! Yeah. It was terrible. He drove onto a baseball diamond during a little league game. Tragedy. Wrote a song about it. Maybe one day you'll hear it."

"Wasn't he going to buy you beer?"

"Well, that was the rumor. But yeah, he was. Fault is entirely on me. I should bought him those wood extensions for the accelerator and *definitely* for the brakes. But it's not all bad. The song is awesome. I'll let you hear it one day."

"Looking forward to that! Loved the last song you sent me!"

"This one's even better! A real classic rock feel. Anyway, enough of your bullshitting! SELL ME A REMOTE-START SYSTEM, BAYIIIIIIIIIIIIIIIIITCH!!!!!!!!!!!!!!!"

Tony Tone laughs very, very hard. It is *extremely* funny. "Just one?"

Randy nods.

"Hmmmm. I had you pegged all wrong."

"How so?" asks Randy. He appears confused, which is rare.

"I don't know. It's just … I don't know, you just seem like a guy with money. Just the way you carry yourself. *Smooth*. You don't walk so much as *glide*. Little things like that."

"Is more than one remote-start system necessary?"

"If you even have to ask …"

Randy ponders this. He strokes his strong chin with his nimble fingers.

"You're right," he exclaims eventually. "*Two* then! Why the fudge not, right?"

"Hail yeah! Now we're talkin'! Whooo! Lettuce don't matter at all to this here Richie Rich!"

"You damn right it doesn't!"

"You know what *does* matter?"

"What?"

"Chrome-rim tire spinners."

"Oooooooooh!" Randy moans, beyond excited.

Tony Tone lets out a laugh. And a huge smile.

This *isn't* rare.

It seems as if *everyone* in Montgomery County Maryland knows and enjoys being around Randy S._____!

And Randy is *a-okay* with that!

Genius is often a beautiful, but odd thing to behold!

The two men get down to the very important business at hand.

[Note: This is Randy, not Noah. I wanted you to see the lyrics I wrote for my song about Lil Mac. It's called "Death Doesn't Die with Death." You can download it by request at Numberonelover453@ yahoo.com for an extremely reasonable $1.99, payable by personalized check and mailed to PO Box 237, Poolesville, Maryland, 20837. Warning: *it's sad.*]

Ice cream comes in all flavors
And so do humans.
Black, white, red, and blue.
Friends ain't no different.
His name was Lil Mac and he had a big-ass heart.
Too bad he had to die.
Miss that lil fucker.
Had a goiter on his neck, twas as hard as rubber.
RIP, little man!
See you on the other side.
And we'll take one more ride.
I can already see your giant-ass grin.
This time, you're gonna strap yourself in.
On your way to buy me some booze
I was way too drunk off the cooze.
You did me a solid. Will see ya in heaven!
Will hand over a tenner.
And we'll call it even.
Accept it. Don't be a fool!
Just be cool.
Should have definitely bought you those
wood extensions for the brakes!
What the hell?
We all make our mistakes!!

--Written by Randy S._____, copyright by Randy S._____, transcribed by Noah B.

Chapter Three:
IT'S *ALL* A PARTY!

The party is in full swing!

Randy is his typical convivial delight, flitting from neighbor to neighbor. A kind word here. A compliment there. The great man is in his element, smack dab within the cozy, fenced-in backyard of his town home. Food is plentiful, the vino is a-flowing, the numerous cans of Natty Boh sunk deep into a large metal bucket filled with *round* cubes with *center holes* (Randy's preference), a folding metal-framed table spread liberally with steamed hard-shell crabs (with their natural "mustard" included), a few key-lime pies from Balducci's, as well as an assortment of other yummy desserts, including a box of Ho-Hos (Randy's absolute fave).

No one is complaining.

"The turnout isn't as great as I was hoping," admits Randy. "But for those who *did* come, they're having the time of their g-damn lives!"

It must be noted that Randy is an extremely well-regarded member of his community. Since 2015, when the development came into being, Randy has proudly served as President of the Fernwood Pines Neighborhood Association.

That is the *top* position.

Randy never expects to give up this position.

As part of his title, Randy hosts an association party at his town home every few months.

"I want to introduce you to someone *very* special," he says. "This is Harriet B._____. She faints and has dizzy spells. An inner-ear disorder. Makes her dizzy. *Always* seasick. I once borrowed her support dog Benedict for the day. Man, that went *bad!*"

"Benedict isn't comfortable around lights or loud noise," explains Harriet, smiling.

"Or strippers sliding down poles," finishes Randy. "Kind of hoping he'd get me in for free. He didn't. Not necessarily his fault. And he forced me to leave early. Took a shit in the handicapped stall. But, man, the girls fucking *loved* him!"

"He came back smelling terribly of smoke," Harriet exclaims, a bit sharply.

"And that's why I bought shampoo," Randy explains, without the slightest tinge of defensiveness. He's just stating a fact. "As good as *new*, right?"

"Right," answers Harriet. "Dandruff shampoo for humans."

"It was cheaper," says Randy. "Where's the little fella now?"

"Not here," says Harriet. "But his rash is beginning to clear."

"Awesome," says Randy, absently. There's a lot on his mind. "*Terrific* news."

"I *did* want to talk to you," continues Harriet.

"Really? For what?" asks Randy, surprised.

"For agreeing to the extension on my backyard fence. You didn't have to do that. I appreciate you allowing me to break the subdivision's bylaws. It was—"

Randy has already moved on.

"Okay, so this is Bam Bam! Why I callin' you Bam Bam, Arnold? Any good reason? Why I do *dat*?!"

A short, balding man—wearing pleated shorts, a long-sleeve blue shirt, and a Washington Nationals visor—stands and wipes his hands on a paper napkin. It's obvious he's exceedingly thrilled to see Randy.

"I don't know," he says, smiling. "I never did find out."

"And you never *will* find out, son!" says Randy, grinning. "You're just Bam Bam. End of da *motherfucking* story! This guy has season tickets to the fucking *Nationals*. Can you believe that?! Hasn't invited me yet, though!"

"I … I split the season with three others at my firm," Arnold sputters, somewhat sheepishly. "My nephews are *huge* fans of Zimmerman, as you know. And I always thought you were more of an O's fan than a …"

"Zimmerman is a chooch," announces Randy. "A $200 million *chooch*! But that's *fine*. I hate National League anyway. I hate watching pitchers hit. Like watching dinosaurs fight with their tiny little arms. Enjoy yourself! Eat whatever you want. Try the slaw. I bought it at the *fancy* Giant on Rockville Pike!"

Bam Bam finishes wiping his hands and then takes a sip of beer.

"Thanks for signing off on my new garage, Randy," he chirps. "You didn't have to do that and I appreciate you overriding the development's bylaws—"

Randy has already moved on. There are *a lot* of people to meet. One is Nora, a thirty-something K Street tax lawyer.

"Hello, Randy," she says.

"Hello, Nora. Did you bring anything? Food? *Drink?*"

"I didn't know I was supposed to," she replies, a bit defensively.

"Would have been *nice*. But that's okay. Eat whatever you want. *Enjoy.*"

Randy strides away and diplomatically whispers: "Can't stand her. All stuck up in the clouds of Academic-ia. I once pissed her off. Asked her what her shaving schedule was. Just trying to make small talk. She's *impossible*. A real wily piece of womanhood. A surly rascal. I was just curious. *Genuinely!* She didn't answer. I wouldn't mind a no, but how about a *something*? She desperately wants to become president here in the development. I said, *No way!* Angling for it. I *know* she is. That will *never* happen. Not a chance. I'll make *sure* of that. Fuck her. *Tony Tone!* My man!"

It's Tony Tone from Absolute Electronix! He's wearing a Giorgio Armani jacket with side zipper pockets. He's sipping on a Natty Boh.

Randy doesn't limit his parties to those who reside in the development.

As anyone would attest, Randy is *extremely* gracious.

"Thanks for coming today, duder!" Randy says.

"Wouldn't miss it for the world! You're my *best* customer!" says Tony Tone.

"You goddamn right!"

"When you coming in next? Missed seeing you this week!"

"No plans. *Busy.*"

Tony Tone looks around. "Okay. But you don't need a musical car horn?"

Randy's attention snaps to. "Musical?"

"Can make 'em play *anything*. Any song you want!"

"Really? *Anything*? Even Jefferson Starship?"

"Hail yeah!"

"Asia?"

"*Anything*, bruv. Come on in! The king in his *goddamn* kingdom!"

"And so the king *shall*. Enjoy the crabs! Got 'em for *half* off!"

Randy glides past a few of his exceedingly happy constituents, including a young woman checking her baby's diaper to see if the baby needs to be changed. This is Holly R._____, who lives down the street.

"Ha! Now *that* looks familiar!" Randy says, mischievously.

"Does it? I didn't know you had a baby, Randy!" Holly answers, barely looking up, concentrating on the diaper change.

"A baby?" asks Randy, genuinely confused.

He confidentially strolls over to an elderly woman. "Okay, so this young lady is Mary Mary. Eighty-five years *young*! Right, Mary Mary?"

"Whaaaaaaaaaaaat?" the woman asks.

"He is asking if you are eighty-five years *old*!" responds a Caribbean-American nurse and attendant, sitting next to her.

"*Young*!" corrects Randy. "Eighty-five years *young*!"

"What?!" Mary Mary screams.

"Nothing, darlin'," says Randy. "Just enjoy the crabs."

"She don' eat 'em," responds the nurse. "She don't eat no shell fish. Nuttin' but cottage cheese!"

"Then why in the fuck is she here?" mutters Randy, before making his way over to a twenty-something holding a crab hammer but with no crabs in sight. The young man is wearing a dress shirt, buttoned all the way to the neck, and a Swatch watch on each wrist, one red, one blue.

"And this very awesome and special dude is Roger but I call him *the Dodger*! Ain't that right, Roger Dodger!"

"That's right!" shrieks Roger Dodger. "I love Randy!"

"Roger Dodger is the *real* deal when it comes to tasks. Ain't that right, Roger?"

"That's right!" yells Roger Dodger. "I shovel snow and I cut grass. I *love* Randy!"

"He really does, that's not a lie," agrees Randy. "Refuses to take any money. Just hugs. And hard candy, which I fucking hate anyway. Works out well! Good thing his parents are rich. *Right, Roger Dodger*?!"

"*Randy*!" yells Roger Dodger. "I love Randy so so *so* much!"

"Okay, see you tomorrow, Dodger," exclaims Randy.

"Gonna spray down your dehumidifier filters!" screams the Dodger. "I love Randy!"

Randy walks away. "About as sharp as a medicine ball," he mumbles. "A real man about Down's, if you know what I mean. A true rumdum dummy. But works harder than anyone I know. And even a few I don't."

Randy makes his way over to another very grateful neighbor and guest. "And this here would be Leigh C._____. This crazy dude claims he's Taiwanese but I can't for the life of me see that. And I'm *real* good at guessing! Where's your gal pal, Leigh?"

"My wife, Betsy. She … she's under the weather," responds Leigh. "But I'm having a wonderful, *wonderful* time. Thank you for the invite. And thank you for allowing us to build a backyard porch beyond the suggested regulations."

"You got it," pronounces Randy. "Anything, my man. By the way, did I ever tell you about the McHilson twins? One was blond, one brown-haired? Both liked to suck on my sweaty, expanding pear? That's what I call my cock! *Ha*!"

"Yes you have, yes," laughs Leigh. "*Very* good."

"Leigh is an important guy at the CIA," explains Randy, proudly. "A real spook. But I sometimes get the feeling that he only shows up to my parties because I allow him to break the bylaws here in the development!"

"*Private sector,*" corrects Leigh. "Nothing covert about my job, sir. Communication satellites at various telecommunications firms. And I would come to your parties anyway, Randy! You know that!"

"*Military* satellites," states Randy. "And I was just kidding. Of course you'd show! I just wish your hot wife would also show now and again! She's white. Just kidding! She's not that hot! But she *is* white! Ha *ha*!"

A look crosses Leigh's face but it's difficult to decipher. "Very nice party, Randy. *Thank you.*"

Leigh retreats back to a white plastic stackable chair to sit alone.

"I could swear to god he's Japanese and not Taiwanese. There *is* an easy way to tell. But I'm not telling. Good party trick. C'mere, I want to show you something."

Randy climbs the stairs up to his second-floor wooden deck, then opens the sliding-glass door that leads into his $1.5 million town home. He strides into his very modern kitchen, all appliances stainless and sleek, all top of the line. Randy points to a large cereal dispenser, made entirely out of plastic tubing and duct tape. It takes up nearly the entire kitchen counter.

"That's my new 18-shooter cereal dispenser! The type you'd find at the fanciest of colleges. *Bigger*! Each hose is *different*. I made it myself. At this point it's just a prototype. Cheerios. Honey Nuts. *Froot Loops*. No one's made it this big before. I'm gonna copyright it. Gonna call it the Cereal Killah. *Incredible*."

Randy spreads his arms wide.

"Take notice! Do you see anything missing? Can you guess? In the kitchen? No? Yes? I'll *tell* you! I don't have an oven or a goddamn microwave. It gives ladies the wrong idea. I don't cook. *They* can do that! At *their* houses. Better yet, we eat out. I'm a huge fan of *restaurant quality* food. You're welcome."

Randy walks past Mam-Mam's old rattan chair in the living room, past an empty lizard terrarium filled with unwashed golf course pebbles, as well as a tiny plastic McMansion that a lizard used to live within, and then over to a large bookcase, packed with books.

"Don't go nuts. These are fake books. Just for show. I bought them from the same place where Ikea gets their fake books. So I can do *this*."

Randy easily slides the book case to the side. Behind the bookcase is a hidden door with an electronic entry pad.

It's all very James Bond.

Randy types his special six-number code into the pad (696969), a beep resounds, and the door swings open with a lovely click.

Randy enters.

"Don't panic but this is my panic room."

Randy waits for the laugh that he's certain will arrive.

When it doesn't, he continues: "Ain't it something? I'm at peace here. Not a soul to bother me." He points to the flat-screen television, next to a poster of the 1990s hard rock group Tin Machine, one of Randy's favorites. "That poster is signed by all of the band's members except David Bowie. It's *very* valuable.

"So this is where I do my best sex watching," he continues. "*Total* privacy. Take a seat on the carpet. The room, as you can see, is empty except for the TV. I don't want it *too* comfortable. Otherwise I'd *never* leave!"

Randy picks up a very large remote and presses "ON." A video appears on the flat-screen. It's paused.

Randy presses "PLAY."

At first, the video is difficult to make out. It's grainy. It's dark. One can see pinpoints of lights flickering, all in the distance, hazy.

"Ocean City. 2015. Remember that legal case I couldn't tell you about? No? Maybe I didn't. Well, I can now tell you *everything*. I rented a video drone from a guy named Boardwalk Billy. Flew it above the beach at night. Saw some things no one else ever has. I couldn't believe how great it was. I later had to lie: '*Why no, mister judge, I wasn't shooting a porno! It was a documentary on Ocean City. About the tourism industry! Yes, at night. I shot it a night in case the drone fell!*'

"Right. I'm being sarcastic. Here we go. College students fuck-ing. It's a documentary. I turned on the infrared. Green shadows going at it. But the *clarity*! You're the first person to ever see this. It's gonna be huge. Voyeur is *huge*. And porn parodies. They're popular again! I mean, I've been banging on that there tambourine for years! Everything old is *new* again!"

Randy takes a seat on the plush rug. He is an auteur admiring his own work, knowing every delicious detail, mouthing along to the sexy dialogue that he imagines could very well be taking place on the sand between the various young lovers.

The video makes more sense now.

It quickly becomes erotic.

"My legal troubles are over. Pure pleasure from here on out. Going to sell this one at conventions and online through my Facebook page. I can see it becoming an underground hit. I have so many movie ideas. I *will* make something soon! God, I have such a *fever* to create! I'M A-BURSTIN! This movie is just the beginning! I GOT THE *FEVER*!"

In his backyard, Randy's neighbors are partying their asses off in the sun, amidst a feast of a lifetime.

Here inside Randy's cozy panic room—where he is cool and safe, comfortably hidden away from any prying eyes and potential enemies, away from any unwanted attention that a local "character" must have to deal with on a daily basis—Randy, like most soothsayers, is talking only of the future, speaking only the truth.

Pure pleasure from here on out.

It is a claim that's difficult to dispute.

Randy continues watching his cinematic masterpiece, eyes wide open, mouth agape, mouthing along in time.

Strong jawed and suave.

Hours later, long after all of the guests have left, he will still be going at it.

If it wasn't before, it's now more than clear to anyone willing to take a deep and long look: Randy's commitment to the arts is something to behold!

An Outsider's Perspective!

Sarah Markus, reporter, the *Potomac Almanac*: "Is Randy really writing a memoir? That's interesting. Randy … he's very colorful. There's always an adventure swirling around Randy. Off the top of my head, we've written about Randy shooting a rifle in the air to celebrate the Redskins beating the Cowboys. The bullet landed in an animal sanctuary, killing a lamb. There was the time he was arrested for sitting on a hill with binoculars watching the prom kids arriving to their party. There was that time he set up a protest tent outside a Bubba Gump's for a week because they no longer served the 'Mama's Bread Pudding.' He wanted to sue but even the ACLU talked him out of that one. There's the whole American Girl Doll store thing with the ACLU. That's still going on. I don't know. Is Randy really writing a memoir? He does visit sick kids in the hospital without their or their parents' permission, so there's that, I suppose."

RANDY'S LEAST-FAVORITE PEOPLE

Tony Kornheiser. He's an asshole.

Manager at the Baskin-Robbins at Congressional Mall.

That's it.

.

Chapter Four:
HALLOWEEN TIME!

There is a nip in the air. Fall has arrived.

"Fall is my favorite time of year," Randy declares. "Gets darker earlier. That's when Randy Dandy really come out to play. I'm like a cool vampire. Not one of those old ones. I hate vampires who are eight hundred years old. They're annoying, like elderly people. They can't figure out computers or electronics. They can't change their clocks when it's that time of year. They have to leave the house to buy diabetic socks. *Ha*! I'm *kidding*! But that would make for a *great* comic-strip! Write that down."

Randy pulls out his keychain with the bottle opener attached. He presses the remote-start system for his 2010 Hummer H3. This was the last year Hummer produced the automobile, which Randy finds very, very sad. He considers this Hummer a "lost classic."

Outside, the Hummer hums beautifully to life. It's a magical sound. The vanity plates read RNDY84, the year of Randy's birth. Randy likes to sometimes joke that his glorious birth occurred within a golden eagle's nest—three dozen feet across—set into a shallow cavity on top of a snow-covered mountain. In reality, Randy's birth took place on the third floor of a hospital in Alexandria, Virginia.

Randy walks out into the cool air and slips into his Hummer. He flicks on his Kenwood DPX302U CD receiver player and sings along to "Take a Look at Me Now" by Phil Collins, but with his own delightful lyrics added:

> *"Take a look at my balls,*
> *Well, there's just a solid sack …*
> *And there's nothing left here to remind you*
> *To take a look at this big ol' sack …"*

Randy giggles. "I'm *great* at song parody." He switches to another song on the CD and clears his throat.

> *"Stink so good!*
> *C'mon, baby, let it stink so good!*
> *Sometimes a hole don't stink like it should!*
> *Bump bump! Stink so good!"*

Randy pumps his fist.

"That's John Mellencamp 'Hurt So Good'! How *great* is that? I got in touch with John. Asked him permission to sell this. He never got back to me. Wouldn't mind a 'no,' just a something. *Asshole.*

"Yeah, that was frustrating. Maybe Goose gave me the wrong email. Maybe John doesn't have an AOL account. I don't know.

"I can be as serious as the next guy, believe me," he continues. "But I do adore humor. Fucking *love* it."

As if to prove this, Randy breaks into a parody of the Frank Sinatra hit "New York New York: *Start spreading your legs … I'm coming today … I want to be between ya now … your ass, my face!"*

He laughs.

"I can safely say that my humor IQ is in the *genius* range.

"I will give you a specific example: I've always dreamed of writing and drawing a hugely popular comic-strip. I *love* newspaper funnies. If I had to list my favorites, they'd be *Zits, Funky Winkerbean, Snuffy Smith, Momma*. Momma reminds me of Mam-Mam. Just the way she looks. And her attitude. Oh, and I fucking love *Andy Capp*.

"They don't make comics like *Andy Capp* anymore. They can't.

Wouldn't be allowed. The *Post* got rid of it. It's about *real* life. It's about how a man struggles with being married. I've been married twice. I can tell you that it's spot on. *Andy Capp* is an *extremely* realistic look at marriage and dealing with difficult women. Mrs. Capp is always raising her rolling pin but Andy is way too much a man to stand for it. He'll just turn around and head right back to the bar.

"My first marriage was to the daughter of the owner of a TCBY on Rockville Pike. I used to call the place *Totally Crummy Bitch of a Yob.* I worked there for two years when I was twenty-eight to thirty. I clawed my way up to assistant manager. It wasn't easy. But I *did* it.

"How do I put this delicately? I'm trying to be dignified about this. Sara was fucking crazy. Off her lally-looper! Somewhere over the brainbow! Elevator never reaching the stars!

"She had real mental issues and we didn't connect. She came to believe that I had planted a bug in her brain. I only *claimed* that I had planted a bug in her brain. It's not like I would know how to technically do that! I wouldn't call Radio Shack and ask, *'Hey! I'm looking to implant a bug in my wife's brain! Can you help? What type of battery should I use? Double or triple A?'* I had the marriage annulled after a few weeks. She was nice. She now owns an Edible Arrangements. We're still great Facebook friends but, to be honest, she was never on my creative wavelength. I'll give you an example.

"I love zombies. One of my better comic-strip ideas is to draw a family of Zombies called The Zombanskies. They're Zombies but also a typical suburban family. Sara thought the idea was stupid. She didn't want me to spend the $25,000 on hats, T-shirts, dolls. She wanted to spend the money for her mental hospital stays. I tried to explain to her—and I'd do it over and over again—why it was absolutely *necessary* to have this stuff in order to sell the idea to a newspaper syndicate. But she wouldn't listen. Stubborn as all get out! I had another amazing comic idea called *Millennial Blues.* It's like *Cathy* but for Millennials. There's Benny. He's twenty-six. The partier of the bunch. He's a struggling rock musician. Writes a lot of cool lyrics about getting hum-hums in the back booth of a KFC …"

Randy stops talking and practically slaps his forehead. "*Whoa*! I just had another idea for a syndicated comic. It just came to me! I would absolutely love to do a strip on Ayn Rand's writings. I *love* her. I've never read any of her books but I do love her. I agree on a lot. Can you write that down? My hands are sweaty. Yeah, that could work. I also love Dean Koontz. I own all his books. They're in alphabetical order in my living room. Like a real library! What else? Maybe something about Jim Jones. I'm fascinated by that guy's story! All that *power*. Do you know that it was Flavor Aid and not Kool Aid he used? Fucker was too cheap to even use Kool Aid! What a character! That's *good* trivia!

"My second wife, Denise, was nice but the union didn't last long at all. We parted on very good terms, although she did end up getting half of my Redskins collectible cards. That sucks. But we're still incredible Facebook friends. I have *a lot* of amazing Facebook friends. Except for that asshole manager at Baskin-Robbins. I blocked him. Only gives me four or five of those pink spoon samples. I want ten! I *need* ten! It is my *right*! Nazi bastard! I hate him!!!

"Do you want to know how Denise and I met? I was training to be a Navy SEAL. I've always loved those guys—*oh, that's another comic-strip idea*! *That would be awesome!* Team SEAL Six! I'll have to ask the government. Find me the number. I've always wanted to be a SEAL! Ever since *G.I. Jane.* I fucking love that movie! When I was still living on Mam-Mam's farm, I built a replica of a SEAL training course in the back and I'd post Facebook photos of me training. Denise saw the photos and got real excited. We started talking. On our second date, she gave me a 'swish and a wish,' which is when a girl gives you a ham-ham inside a car wash. Got married the next day."

Randy sighs loudly. "I really wanted that marriage to work. I truly and really did. But Denise wasn't into historical role play. I like to play 16th century Australian detectives hunting down Jack the Ripper. Like, *'Excuse me, madam, I am looking for Jack the Ripper and I doth wonder if thee might be of any assistance?'* But I say it in a foreign accent. I then proceed to ask if I can have sex with the prostitute. She's saucy and always says yes. I've found this to be catnip for the kitty cats. Not Denise. *Difficult* Denise!

"She gave me *zero* support. Like when I wanted calf implants, something I've always wanted. Both of my legs, the bottom parts, have always been *way* too thin. To be fair, we were low on dough. She wanted to give all our money to her mother for some type of medical treatment for cancer. I soon quit her and began dating an indoor lacrosse cheerleader, Alexa. That lasted a week. She was crispy but didn't have the mental goods. Denise's mom died."

Randy points to his head.

"God, I have so many ideas. I wrote a porn version of *Groundhog Day* called *Horndog Day*. The character gets laid every goddamn day but in a different way! It's hilarious. And sexy has hell. It *will* get made and soon!

"To get back to *Millennial Blues*, there's the character of Benny, who I've already mentioned, and then there's Stuey, who's twenty-eight. He's the nerd of the group. Loves to read long novels. I can't think of any at the moment. But they're long. There's Becca, twenty-one. Major-league hotty. Stuey has a crush and tries to impress her with his amazing yo-yo tricks. The Captain is thirty-one. Older than the rest. Been around the block. He once got drunk and shaved off all his body hair and then ran into a Red Lobster. I did that once."

Randy makes a "hurry up" motion. "My brain is in overdrive now. I've reached cruising altitude. Or *attitude*. Ha! Have you ever fantasized about having an alien pet? That could make for a cool comic. He'd make my bed. And cook me frozen waffles by just pointing a finger at 'em. And if it was a girl alien, she'd give me a morning yank. I'd tell her, 'Wake me up at a quarter to spank.' And the alien's name would be Maggi.' Do you know what ALF stands for? *A Loving Friend.* He's an alien who fell from the sky. And he has a snappy comeback for *everything!* What a character!

"I can't overwork it or I get the head troubles. Even the most powerful computers are capable of overheating. That's proven. *Maxim* once talked about all of this.

"This is a mix I put together called 'Early Fall.' Spin Doctors. Chris Gaines. Billy Joel. Van Halen. Marcy Playground. Matchbox 20. The classics. The best song is 'Rise Above' from U2's *Spider-Man: Turn Off the Dark.* Fucking *crispy!*"

This afternoon, Randy is on an important quest. It's three days until Halloween. "If I had to list all my favorite holidays, in order, I wouldn't have to think about it hard: it'd be Halloween, right at the top. That's it. The rest are depressing. I do Halloween better than anyone. I make Halloween *my bitch.*

"Every year I have a party and it's always themed. This year's theme is 'Come as You Ain't.' In other words, 'Come as a Different Religion or Race.' I've always wanted to do this. Here's the thing about me: I ain't PC. I have no time for that shit. I'll be going as a Jew. Gal Gadot is Jewish. Wonder Woman. She's got some tig' ol' bitties. I love her. I was raised a Presbyterian. But religion don't matter to me. I don't care what you are. If you're hot, this foreskin wants in."

Billy Joel's "We Didn't Start the Fire" blares forth from the speakers.

"God, I *love* this song. I think it's genius. Do me a favor? You keep pulling that recorder away. Come closer? I want you to catch this. I wrote a more updated version and tried to email Billy Joel the lyrics. I don't mind a 'no.' Would have loved to just know if he ever received it. But I heard nothing. Too much to ask? Maybe his email isn't AOL either. I don't know. Pompous *asshole.*"

Randy begins to sing along to the song, but with his own special, updated lyrics:

Donald Trump, Ronald Regan,
Emma Watson, Saving Private Ryan,
Ted Cruz, Steve Doocy of Fox News,
North Korea, why you cryin',
President Obama, communist,
Born in Africa, why you lyin'?
"Heat of the Moment," "Love in an Elevator,"
"The Boys of Summer,"
"Old Time Rock and Roll,"
"Fat Bottomed Girls,"
"We Can't Dance,"
What else do I have to say? Gotta give these songs a chance!

Clive Cussler, Dean Koontz, Maxim mag,
Lt. Dan's Hot Beef Bites, Bryce Harper's a fag,
Redskins, Capitals, Wizards, O's, Ravens, and Nats,
Take a gander at these zaggy-ass nutz! ...

"That's enough for now," Randy declares, turning down the volume. "That's as far as I've gotten. It's really terrific. But I do have to tweak out the wrinks. Maybe I'll *dark jam* on it tonight."

Randy does his best thinking while soaking in his oversized fiberglass gelcoat bathtub, within his 400 square-foot marbled bathroom.

With the lights turned off—and Randy submerged up to his neck in warm bath water and allowing his thoughts to trek wherever they might desire on any particular day—*anything* can happen. Randy calls this "dark jamming."

"Like a sensory deprivation tank but cheaper."

Randy beeps the Hummer's horn at a driver who has just cut him off. "My new horn plays 'Livin' for the Weekend.' Loverboy. Tony Tone inserted it. Ha! *Inserted* it! That sounds like a joke! It is not."

He sighs and points to a passing car. "Typical. They're fast drivers.

"I'd like to get into the book my thoughts on race," Randy continues, nonchalantly weaving from lane to lane, one hand on the wheel, the other holding a fidget spinner. "I know this can be a bit ticklish but I want it in my own damn memoir. Here's how I feel: no matter *what* we are, be it white or black or yellow or a golden Indian brown, we're *all* fucking annoying. But we're all *equally* annoying. Does that make sense? I annoy *you*. You annoy *me*. He annoys *her*. She annoys *me*. Especially *her* annoying *me*. *Ha*! Punish the deed, not the *breed*!

"I've thought about this a ton. I mean, let's face it, some groups are just more annoying than others. But we're *all* annoying for different reasons. Like, you might not like me because I'm … I don't know … *something*. But I might not like you because you always drive fast or are super good at math without studying, you know? It's all about respect. It ain't your race. It's *grace*."

We're now pulling into a parking lot, which is full. But Randy manages to quickly find a space.

He always does … thanks to his new, even bigger bootleg "handicapped" sign placed around his rearview.

Randy exits his Hummer and locks it with a touch of his keychain.

"I made a Youtube video about race and religion and it went *huge*. A ton of the Super Sensitives were upset but I told the *truth*. That's just the way it *is*."

Randy walks into a store and whistles in surprise. "Wow! *Weird*. I've never been here before. I didn't even know it existed until I Googled the damn thing. *Bizarre*. Where's the salesman? Aren't they supposed to be good at selling?"

A young Hasidic Jew exits from the back of the store and makes his way over to Randy. He exudes a warm presence.

"Welcome! How may I help you this afternoon?"

"Ha," says Randy. "You look awesome! All those layers! Don't you get hot? Especially in the summer?"

"I do just fine," responds the store's owner. "One gets used to it. Are you looking for anything in particular?"

"I am, yes," Randy says. "I have deep respect for the Jews. I'm a big-ass fan of your food, unless it's too salty. I love bagels. Paul Simon. Bruce Springsteen. That movie where the father pretends that the concentration camp is only a game. I *love* that movie! I learned a lot from it. How bad it all was. Adam Sandler is great also! His Hanukkah song is pretty goddamn funny!"

"Okay," replies the store owner.

"I tell you what I do hate, though: nudity in Holocaust documentaries. Totally out of place. So since I respect you so much, and I love the food, except for the salty stuff, I wanna dress as one of you for Halloween."

"One of us?"

"Jewish. But so people can actually tell. Not a hidden one."

"A hidden one?"

"That's right," says Randy, growing frustrated. He always thought Jews were supposed to be "intelligent." *Why is this guy not getting it?*

Randy continues, more slowly: "So it's clear that I'm a Jewish. That's the *point* of the party. Come as something you're *not*."

"Ah, I see," says the store's owner. "You'd like to conflate two thousand years of our history into a Halloween gag. For the amusement of yourself and a few of your friends?"

"Yes! Jesus!" says Randy, exasperated but relieved. "*Exactly.* And neighbors. So am I allowed to look around?"

"You're more than welcome to look around and purchase whatever catches your eye," says the owner, smiling and walking over to the checkout counter. "Spend as much time as you need. I'll be by the register."

Randy makes a motion as if to say, *Well, thank you very much!*, and begins to browse the yarmulke aisle. "Do you have any beanies with the Orioles mascot birdy on it?" Randy asks inquisitively.

"I'm afraid we don't," responds the owner, now on his computer. "You might want to try the Lids at Montgomery Mall."

"But then I wouldn't look so Jewish, would I?" Randy retorts, and returns to his shopping.

Randy has always taken great pride in his Halloween outfits, and this year—the third in a row in which he'll be throwing a party—will be no exception.

"Finding everything you need?" the owner asks a few minutes later, still tapping away on his computer.

Randy nods absentmindedly. "Yeah. I'm *on* it."

Later, after Randy has returned to his town home with $250 worth of Jewish accessories, he will discover that the store owner will have already uploaded numerous photos of Randy shopping. The store's Twitter feed will already have erupted with many comments—more than one hundred—both positive and negative.

But, not surprisingly, the negative remarks won't seem to bother Randy. His inner moral compass is *always* pointed towards *positivity*!

"*All* press is *good* press," Randy will respond. "And I look damn fine in the photos. Almost like a model. Did I ever tell you that I once worked as a famous model? I was the lead actor in the *Mattress Discounters* TV ads. They were huge hits. I was the guy on the mattress with the white boxers and black socks, scissoring my feet in time to the theme song: '*Play* on it, *sleep* on it, *make love* on it!' Anyway, this Twitter attention is awesome! So many more people will come to my Halloween party!"

But that's still a few hours in the future. For now, Randy continues his hunt for that *perfect* beanie.

Within mere moments, Randy finds it.

He gingerly picks up a yarmulke and holds it aloft. "*How perfect is this?* It even has a damn heavy-metal star on it!"

Indeed, the yarmulke has a six-point star on it. The owner snaps a photo.

"Incredible! So so *so* cool! I've *gotta* get one! Shit, I'll get *two*. There's probably a deal. There always is. This is fantastic. I scared people last year. The theme was Quentin Tarantino. Wore an S&M gimp outfit made out of Scuba gear and a red dog treat in my mouth. This is *so* much cooler!"

The owner takes another photo, one of Randy holding the yarmulke high above his head like an angel's halo. Randy is laughing very hard.

"The cherry on top of my delicious Jewish sundae!" Randy exclaims. "Yummy dum *dum*! And *amen*!"

The store owner gives an almost shy smile.

No surprise.

No matter the race, religion or ethnicity, *everyone* adores Randy!

RANDY'S TOP PICK-UP LINES

"Why the long face?"

"You might recognize me from your window."

"Listen, my daughter needs a kidney *real* bad. I'm just kidding!"

"Guess which part of me is prosthetic."

"Can you see my junk through these jeans? *No?* How about *now?*"

"Isn't this place fabulous? Wouldn't you just love to die here?"

"These look like lice bites, right? Apparently, they're only chiggers."

"Let's cut out the bullshit, shall we? How much is this gonna cost me?"

"Do you remember where you were when you first heard the Spin Doctors?"

"Can I touch your secret hair, baby doll?"

"Do my palms smell weird?"

"The Muppets are bullshit, and let me tell you why."

"You look familiar. Didn't we once meet once at a hospital hospice?"

"I really think M. Night Shyamalan is an auteur in the traditional sense."

"They're night-vision goggles, and no, I won't be removing them."

Chapter Five:
DEEP STATE!

The November morning dawns clear and bright, a brisk wind blowing in from the southeast.

Inside Randy's town home, on the other hand, things are only heating up. Within his development, political intrigue abounds.

He's none too happy about it.

Randy peeks out his bedroom window.

"That fucking bitch! *Who?!* Who the fuck *else*?! She lives across the street. Nora! I *hate* her! And she hates me! Ever since I backed into her Mercedes with my sit-down mower. I was drunk! And I offered to pay it all back. In installments. But she wanted it all at once. And I refused! *That's* who!"

He paces.

"Nora *definitely* took that photo on Halloween and sent it to the *Potomac Almanac.* I *know* it was her! What balls! And the TV news. Every time they arrive with all their cameras and trucks, the neighbors get all worked up. Okay, so I dressed as a Jew for Halloween. No one does that?!"

Randy's long-time loyal escort, April, reclines on a huge, round, king-size bed, watching *Grown-Ups 2* on Randy's 48-inch-flat-screen. She's laughing very hard. Every so often, especially when Randy needs a mental boost, she will pipe up with a line or two of much-needed support: "*Fuck* 'em, Randy. Why don't you just *fuck* 'em *all*? Shit, I *know* I *would* for the right amount!" She laughs, and yet her attention is diverted back to the movie.

It's one of her all-time favorites.

"Would love to," responds Randy, patiently. "But I'm the

president of this here development. I built this place with my own hands. Or paid for it with my own hands. Or with Mam-Mam's hands. Or money. And I have no intention of ever giving that up. I'm president for life. It's a fucking *coup*! They—the *other* side, the *evil* side—they just want to elect their own president. *Unacceptable*! They'll have to *kill* me first!"

Randy is pacing within his inner-most lair, his ultra-designed bedroom. On the walls hang "simulated original" art pieces by well-regarded artists Bob Ross and Thomas Kinkade.

Also on the walls are sheets from Randy's infamous paper towel collection. "I should have seen this coming. I *know* there've been whispers. Layer upon layer of betrayal. I *hate* whispers. I sensed something amiss when no one showed up for the damn Halloween party. Probably still upset I got them all sick from those half-off crabs at the last meeting!"

"It's pronounced *coo*. Not *coop*," says April, a bit pointedly.

"Gee. Someone's in a *mood*," says Randy patiently.

"You know what?" asks April.

"What?" says Randy.

"Go fuck your asshole! *That's* what!"

"No! *You* go fuck my asshole! *Fuck* I pay you for?"

"Shut the fuck up," says April, more loudly than necessary. "Just shut the fuck up!"

"I need this shit. For $300 an hour. Fucking raised her rates on me. We're in the Fantasy Land of Estrogen-onia here! *Balls*!"

That nobody showed up to Randy's Halloween party the previous week isn't entirely true. Roger Dodger—dressed as a middle-class African-American businessman—arrived at Randy's front door, and Randy, dressed as an Orthodox Jew, greeted him most graciously, with a tip of the ol' six-starred beanie.

After a photo of the two was surreptitiously (and possibly illegally) taken by a neighbor, Roger Dodger entered the house and ate cheese puffs for a few hours. He headed back home at 9:30 P.M. The photo and subsequent article later appeared on the front page of the *Potomac Almanac*, above the fold. Much was made of the fact that Randy is not Jewish, Roger Dodger not African-American.

April laughs. "This is *so* funny!" she says, referring to the scene in which Adam Sandler farts into his hands and then spastically spreads the joy over to his friends.

"Glad you're having fun," says Randy, "but I need a *brain* here. And you're on my goddamn time and my damn god dime."

"*Damn god dime?*" repeats April. "What does *that* mean?"

"It means that I'm paying you on my dime! Your god *damn* time! *Jesus!*"

"You're not paying me, Randy," says the Dodger. "Could you pay *me* dimes?! I *love* dimes!"

"I *am* paying you, dude. Right? I'm paying you with goddamn *hugs*! Right? Cash comes *down the road*. I've told you that. I'll eventually owe you like $20 for all your hard work. You'll *get* it."

"Can you pay me now?" asks the Dodger to his hero. "In *hugs*?"

"Um, no. Sorry," says Randy, meaning it. "I don't have any change. How about a tiny bit of Bitcoin?"

The Dodger looks sad.

April sits up. "Remind me again? What's happening? Why are you so upset?"

"I am the president!" yells Randy. "I am the fucking president of this development! *Capiche?*"

"*Capeeeeeesh*," responds April. "Geez!" Her attention returns to the movie. "Oh, this part is funny, too! Adam Sandler sneezes into a baby chicken's rear end!"

"Forget it," says Randy, leaving the bedroom. "Refried confusion. Typical. I'm going downstairs. Meeting's in ten minutes. Gotta figure out a game plan here!"

"Me too!" screams the Dodger. "*Downstairs!*"

Both head to the first floor of the town home. Randy walks off and begins to pace, going over the speech he's about to give. It could be the most important speech of his entire life. He *has* to get this right. He is a *perfectionist*. When he looks up, he finds Roger Dodger sticking his thumb into the base of a lit candle and delicately licking the hot wax off his finger.

"Dude!" Randy screams toward Roger Dodger. "Guests are coming any minute! What are you *doing*?! Let's *go* here!"

"Okay, Randy!" says the Dodger, wiping the wax off on his jeans. "Okay dokie!"

"*Okie* dokie!" corrects Randy. "It's *okie*! How many times?!"

A familiar melody is heard. It's the doorbell, chiming "Some Like It Hot" by the successful 1980s supergroup The Power Station. Tony Tone has just installed it. Randy takes this moment to point to his smile, now fresh on his face, as if to say: "Folks! It is *showtime*!"

Randy opens the door. There stands Arnold, otherwise known as "Bam Bam." Randy and Bam Bam greet each other warmly. This is Randy's way. He is an *impeccable* host, even when not in the best of moods—a rarity.

Randy makes it clear to Bam Bam that there are plenty of cheese puffs in the plastic bowl on the kitchen counter. Also, unused Halloween candy still in their unopened bags. "All you can eat!" he generously states. "And I cannot wait for you to hear my Rock and Roll Meeting Mix! Took days to put together but it's *really* gonna set the festive mood!"

The living room fills with Randy's neighborhood constituents. By 7:16, it's standing room only.

Except for Randy, who's sitting in Mam-Mam's old rattan chair, fingers clasped in front of him in a steeple, wearing mirrored sunglasses. He nods. It's difficult to read his expression.

Just the way he wants it.

He begins his speech. It's gorgeously written.

But, more than anything, it's the *way* in which Randy delivers it that makes it an instant classic:

"Welcome. And I say that to *all*. Not to just the few. You might have seen a few photos of me in this week's *Potomac Almanac*. It doesn't take an Encyclopedia Brown to figure out who *took* it—" Randy shoots a quick glare in Nora's direction "—but since I'm such a compassionate person, I will *overlook* those photos."

He clears his throat for dramatic effect and adjusts his mirrored sunglasses so that they cover even more of his eyes.

"What I am *not* willing to overlook, however, are the rumors I've been hearing from a very special source—" Randy winks at Roger Dodger "—who has kindly informed me that there have been malicious rumors that a certain someone—and that would be me—needs to resign his position as president of this here neighborhood association. This would be the neighborhood I built with my own hands. Or with Mam-Man's hands. Or money."

He pauses.

"Sad."

He pauses again.

"*Really* sad."

Harriet B._____ starts: "Randy, it's not that we don't appreciate all the amazing and superb work you've done as president of this association—"

Randy holds up his hand. Harriet stops talking.

"I shall now *officially* open the floor up to comments from my constituents," Randy patiently states. "Go ahead, Harriet. You have my permission now."

Properly rebuked, Harriet B._____ begins yet again: "Randy, it's not that we don't appreciate all the superb work you've done as president of this association … but we sort of feel that we might need … some *fresh* blood."

Now Leigh C._____ jumps in. "Randy, you've done—I mean,

are doing—an amazing job! But … there seems to be a disconnect between what we want to achieve here and how you wish to … lead."

Still no expression from Randy. He's playing it *very* cool, as is his wont.

"And besides," chirps Bam Bam, "you're so busy on your … inventions and artistic projects. Aren't you? Maybe this will give you more time to focus on your inventions? And your art projects?"

Randy remains quiet. Finally, after seemingly a full minute, he shakes his head and turns to Roger Dodger. "Roger Dodger. What do you think of all this? It seems to me as if they don't want me any more as their leader."

Roger Dodger beams. "I *love* you, Randy!"

"I know you do, Roger," says Randy. "But it seems that the rest of this development … does *not*. And what might *you* think, Mary Mary? What are your thoughts on all this?"

"She don tink nuttin," responds her Caribbean-American nurse. "She don even wanta be here. And me neitha!"

"Old nanny goat," says Randy.

"Come on now," says Miss Y._____, a middle-aged woman, meekly. This is not her best look. "Let's not get overly dramatic. We just wish to elect a new development association president. And we have the majority. That's it. Simple."

"Incredible," says Randy, sadly. "After all I've given you. How very much I wanted to give you all the good life here. Not to mention *bigger* backyards and *higher* fences. Yeah."

"Oh, come on!" says a thirty-something in a blue suit and red tie. "Let's just elect a new development president and get the hell out of here already. I mean, *really*!"

"I can't even leave the house without the goddamn TV cameras following me everywhere!" says another man. "My daughter in Silver Spring! Keeps seeing me on the news! Can you imagine? And because of what? *No more attention, Randy! We're done with it*!"

"Oooh. Little man make big stinky!" says Randy, voice rising. "Betrayal. *Duplicity*. You refused to come to my Halloween party. You would have all enjoyed it so much. So very much."

"He's still wearing a yarmulke," someone—it can't be clear quite who—interjects lamely.

"My *lucky* heavy metal beanie," corrects Randy. "It brings me luck. Or is *supposed* to. Not today, though."

"C'mon, man," says a muscular, bald-headed young man in a tight tank top. Another bald-headed man stands next to him. They look to be a couple. "Don't start with this shit. You're lucky we're not kicking your ass out."

"Not possible," declares Randy, all cool. "I bequeefed this land to you. From my loins."

"Be*queath*ed," corrects a man named Stuart Z._____, a banker from Australia.

"Joke," says Randy. "*Queef.* Means 'pussy fart.' Was a *joke*! Relax, you Austrian!"

"*Australian*," corrects the man.

"A plate of biscuits and a bag of squirrel gravy! Fuck's the difference? Always with the goddamn corrections!" says Randy.

"You've done *nothing*," says Mrs. T____. "Absolutely nothing! Except bring shame to this development. And especially with this most recent hubbub!"

"I brought you *nothing*?" asks Randy. "That doesn't even make *insane* sense! Are you *kidding*?! You mean no funny flags waving proud? Just look around! Are you *blind*!"

"We don't want your stupid flags!" screams a young mother, holding her baby close. "We never *wanted* the flags! We never wanted the funny mailboxes! It's not funny. It's not cute! We don't want *any* of it! Like being forced to come to your stupid-ass parties and kiss your stupid ass!"

"Speaking of ass, your baby just shat. Or was that Mary-Mary?"

Randy impishly declares.

"Right," says one of the bald-headed young men. "You wrote the damn bylaws anyway. Why do we have to grovel to you so that you can break them for us?"

"Your *type*," says Randy. "Your type is really *something*, I tell ya."

"Excuse me?" says the bald-headed young man.

"We're *all* annoying," explains Randy. "No matter *who* we are."

"Fuck does that mean?" asks the other bald-headed man.

"Come on. Don't make it hard for me," says Randy, very patiently.

"No, go on," says one of the bald-headed men. "Cause we're gay? And a couple?"

"*What*?! That's homophobic! No!" screams Randy. He means it. "No. What I'm saying is, We're *all* annoying. No matter *who* we are. Or who we're fucking."

"Dear Lord," says Mrs. T._____. "You know what? I have to attend my daughter's concert. Enough of this crap. Let's vote."

Randy's cellphone rings.

The ringtone is Survivor's classic 1982 mega hit, "Eye of the Tiger."

It is one of Randy's all-time favorites. Another song by Survivor, "American Heartbeat," is Randy's all-time official "stomach crunch tune."

"Probably the damn press," says Mrs. T._____.

Randy shoots her a glare. "Actually, it's my dermatologist. With the test results. But thanks for *guessing*. I'm being sarcastic. But not about the dermatologist. Or the test results. Pre spring-break tradition. I'll get to it later."

"Let's end this. *Now*!" says a man from the back of the room. He looks officious. "Who here would like for Nora to become the next development president to commence immediately? Say 'aye.'"

"Aye!" screams the room.

"And who here would prefer Randy to maintain his position as president of this development?"

"Yah!" yells Roger Dodger. "Hoo-*rah*!"

"Who?" asks Mary Mary to her Caribbean nurse. "*Whaaaaaaaaat*?"

"And that settles it," says the officious man. "Nora, *congratulations*! You are officially this development's new president!"

"Abominable, man," mumbles Randy. "Fucking goddamn *abominable*."

Turning to April, who has just wandered into the meeting, Randy declares, "Hey! Just in time! *Thanks* for the help. I'm being sarcastic."

"I know you are," April replies, grabbing a handful of cheese puffs and making an immediate U-turn and heading straight back up to finish *Grown-Ups 2*.

Within minutes (three and a half to be exact), Randy—still in his chair—and Roger Dodger—still smiling—are the only two left in the room. All of Randy's former constituents have cleared out in a most orderly fashion.

"Boy oh boy! They all left *real* fast!" states the Dodger. "*Wow*!"

"The devils always do," explains Randy.

Roger Dodger looks frightened. "They ... they were *devils*?"

"Relax, idiot," says Randy patiently. "Just *assholes*."

Roger Dodger shrugs. "I love you, Randy. I love you so so *so* much."

"We've been so betrayed," says Randy. "So very betrayed. But it's okay. Blood on my knife or shit on my dick, I will collect what I am owed."

April's voice can be heard calling from the upstairs deluxe bedroom: "*Thirsty*! Diet Mountain Dew! In a *clear* glass! And a straw! Just the way I *like* it! Get it! *Now*!"

"So very betrayed."

"*Get me my beverage! Now*!!!!!!"

"So very betrayed."

"BEVERAGE! NOW!!!!!"

"She's mad! Wowy zoway!" says the Dodger.

Randy, a bit tired from his very busy evening, says, "It's wowy zowie. Zow-*ie,* Dodger. Zow-*ie*. It has to rhyme, idiot."

"Sorry, Randy!"

Randy's cellphone rings. "Eye of the Tiger."

"Dermatologist," says Randy. "Will get it later. Can't be worse than last year's. Groin's *still* on fire."

The two friends go on munching cheese puffs, lost equally in their own thoughts.

They have so very much to think about.

Two men working at the very top of their intelligence on extremely important matters!

An Outsider's Perspective!

Jason Melcher, Rockville, Maryland copyright attorney: "Randy. Randy S._____. Yes, I know Randy. I've ... worked with Randy. Randy is ... unique. He has a lot of ideas for inventions. Has zero problem calling at all hours. Some of those I helped copyright? Well, off the top of my head, a lazy-eye patch with the Aerosmith tongue logo on it. A Van Halen inspired carpal tunnel splint. Mud flaps on a wheelchair. He wanted them to read: MY OTHER RIDE IS YOUR MOM! I don't think any of these have seen the light of day. Those hospital automatic soap foaming dispensers for the car, especially after touching a toll worker's hand. EZ Pass might have ruined that one. A fleshlight surrounded with fake, soft hair but not too much hair. This is for a book? Lord. He's really writing a book? I'll be damned. What else did he invent? I'm trying to remember. Um, a vending machine that dispenses tiny cards with funny jokes on them. A cough lozenge that tastes like chicken fingers. So many inventions. A Lucite toilet seat with live goldfish inside. Not every inventor can be an Edison, I guess. Ape chauffeurs. He wanted apes to drive him around. I don't know how familiar Randy is with simians. Is Randy really writing a book? An actual book? I'll be goddamned."

RANDY'S FAVORITE ALL-TIME BOOKS

Pacific Vortex! by Clive Cussler

The Mediterranean Caper by Clive Cussler

Iceberg by Clive Cussler

Raise the Titanic! by Clive Cussler

Vixen by Clive Cussler

Night Probe! by Clive Cussler

Deep Six by Clive Cussler

Cyclops by Clive Cussler

Treasure by Clive Cussler

Dragon by Clive Cussler

Sahara by Clive Cussler

Inca Gold by Clive Cussler

Shock Wave by Clive Cussler

Flood Tide by Clive Cussler

Atlantis Found by Clive Cussler

Serpent by Clive Cussler

Blue Gold by Clive Cussler

Fire Ice by Clive Cussler

White Death by Clive Cussler

Lost City by Clive Cussler

Polar Shift by Clive Cussler

The Navigator by Clive Cussler

Medusa by Clive Cussler

Devil's Gate by Clive Cussler

The Storm by Clive Cussler

Zero Hour by Clive Cussler

Ghost Ship by Clive Cussler

The Pharaoh's Secret by Clive Cussler

Nighthawk by Clive Cussler

The Rising Sea by Clive Cussler

Sea of Greed by Clive Cussler

Valhalla Rising by Clive Cussler

Trojan Odyssey by Clive Cussler

Black Wind by Clive Cussler

Treasure of Khan by Clive Cussler

Arctic Drift by Clive Cussler

Crescent Dawn by Clive Cussler

Poseidon's Arrow by Clive Cussler

Havana Storm by Clive Cussler

Odessa Sea by Clive Cussler

Celtic Empire by Clive Cussler

Dragonfly by Dean Koontz

Invasion by Dean Koontz

Prison of Ice by Dean Koontz

Night Chills by Dean Koontz

The Face of Fear by Dean Koontz

The Vision by Dean Koontz

False Memory by Dean Koontz

From the Corner of His Eye by Dean Koontz

One Door Away from Heaven by Dean Koontz

By the Light of the Moon by Dean Koontz

The Face by Dean Koontz

The Taking by Dean Koontz

Life Expectancy by Dean Koontz

Velocity by Dean Koontz

The Husband by Dean Koontz

The Good Guy by Dean Koontz

The Darkest Evening of the Year by Dean Koontz

Your Heart Belongs to Me by Dean Koontz

Relentless by Dean Koontz

Breathless by Dean Koontz

Darkness Under the Sun by Dean Koontz

What the Night Knows by Dean Koontz

The Moonlit Mind by Dean Koontz

Shadow Street by Dean Koontz

Wilderness by Dean Koontz

Innocence by Dean Koontz

The Neighbor by Dean Koontz

The City by Dean Koontz

Ashley Bell by Dean Koontz

The Funhouse by Dean Koontz

Basically, anything by Dean Koontz or Clive Cussler

Also, anything by Ayn Rand

Collections of newspaper comics

Cliff Notes to the Bible

Chapter Six:
A MOST FESTIVE CELEBRATION
WITH TERRIFIC FRIENDS!

It's Thanksgiving eve, a few weeks since the presidency was stolen out from under Randy by nefarious means.

The Mustang's Gentlemens Club in Hyattsville is feeling its *true* holiday spirit!

Celebratory yellow and green streamers hang cheerfully from the dropped ceiling. "Happy Turkey Hour" signs abound. The strippers are gaily dolled up as early American settlers and sexy Native-American princesses. Close to the entrance, just next to the jukebox that blasts holiday classics, sits a delicious and ample Thanksgiving spread, complete with sliced-turkey sandwiches, microwavable mashed potatoes with packaged gravy, and an unlimited supply of all the BBQ Dipsy Doodles one could possibly consume. For dessert, a large plastic bowl filled with Pepperidge Farm Pumpkin Cheesecake Soft Dessert Cookies.

Heaven.

Randy sits in front of the main stage, a six-by-six-foot raised platform, watching his favorite stripper, Becki, gyrate to the sounds of "Jive Turkey" by the Ohio Players, a band Randy does not enjoy because they are "too brassy."

"April and I decided to call it quits," says Randy over the thumping loud speakers. "We're still really good Facebook friends but we're no longer officially a client and escort couple." Magnanimously, Randy concludes with: "I wish her the very best. One of the greatest joys of my life was watching how close she became with my hundreds of hermit crabs."

Randy takes an ample bite out of his yummy turkey sandwich. He's thrilled to be celebrating this very special Thanksgiving in such a cheerful, jovial environment.

And yet ... there is a certain *something* that still seems to be missing.

"I think I was maybe telling you earlier about my epiphany," exclaims Randy, "but I never got around to finishing because you interrupted me. It occurred to me that I do need to pop out of a *thing*. I'm not sure what you would call it. A depression? A dip? Maybe. Only then can I move *forward*."

Randy sips his mug of Natty Boh. "What I really need right now is to bring this whole thing full circle. Only *good* things can come from this.

"I'm in a negative spiral. The universe clearly ain't going my way."

As if to refute this, Randy's favorite strip-club DJ, Carl the Great, kicks the holiday eve off with exciting Thanksgiving-infused announcements:

"Happy *Turkey Hour*! *Half off* lap rides! *Dark* meat! *White* meat! *Red* meat! Gonna make you *real* sleepy! Women with all the *trim-* mings! Pilgrims, you *red*-day?!"

Randy finishes his Thanksgiving sandwich, wipes his face with a yellow paper napkin, and takes one last swig of Natty. He points to a stripper standing by a small area that's been enclosed with a shower curtain. The curtain is see-through and features decals of tropical fish swimming through a garden of colorful coral.

It's *very* festive.

"I'm hoping that this Injun will accept my wampum. I *love* the VIP section. I don't like the riff raff in the normal area. Reminds me of Ocean City in the winter. Low-rent Larrys. Honky Henrys. I'm *better* than that. That's why I dig O.C. in the summer. How many of these other losers—"

Randy points to the five men sitting in cheap vinyl seats

surrounding the raised makeshift pallet stage that's attached with glued-on paper pumpkins.

"—have written hundreds of songs, thousands of poems, and a play about Dennis Rodman visiting South Korea? Oh, I'm guessing ... not *many*.

"Or invented more than one hundred products? Did I tell you about any of them? Like my SAFE SIT app. Say you're sitting next to a minority on the Metro. You're not so sure they're safe. You take a photo of the guy. *Secretly*. I'd suggest doing so quickly without them noticing. Like you would with a voyeur sex shot. The photo is then automatically uploaded to a national criminal database using facial technology. Then either 'SAFE' or 'DANGEROUS' will come up on the screen. Apple knows all about this. Also the Department of Defense. I'm still waiting to hear back from both. It'll save a lot of lives. It's *that* simple.

"Another app I invented: WHERE THE SUN DON'T SHINE. Say you're on the Metro or in a car about to take a trip. What side of the car is the sun going to be obnoxiously flashing into? Using GPS and your eventual destination, this'll tell you. The sun is fine but not for more than an hour. Then my psyche hurts.

"I came up with another app called OKCupid PLUS. It's no surprise that most of the women on OKCupid are hideous. I once saw a midget. A fucking midget! I love midgets for fun—if they're riding on the shoulders of normal people or in a Van Halen video. Loved Lil Mac obviously! Until he died in that car accident. *But to date?* Come on. I've seen a fatso with one leg. I guess it's not all bad: she would have only weighed more with it. *Whistle before you explode so I can get out of the room, right*? This app will plug directly into your regular OKCupid account and weed out all the uglies. And then contact the hot Bettys and automatically send them a pre-written message: *I saw you on OKCupid. What up girl?! How is your week going? What are you doing? Do you like beer? How about television?*

"I sent it to OKCupid, but haven't heard back. I wouldn't mind a no, but I would like to hear back. One more app, BAR NONE. You're at a bar. You've run out of things to talk about. You don't have your yo-yo. You've forgotten your magic tricks. You don't know a damn thing about the current political situation. So what do you do? *What do you say?*"

Randy waits for an answer that doesn't arrive.

"You go to BAR NONE and you input information on the Betty you're trying to impress. Age, ethnicity, height, weight, looks. Out pops the *perfect* small-talk suggestion. It's specifically tailored to your situation. 'Are you a C or a double B cup?' Or 'Did you know it wasn't Kool-Aid that Jim Jones used to kill his followers? It was Flavor Aid?' Women *love* that sort of shit!"

Ideas are flowing.

"I invented a *ton* of stuff! Flavored sex lubrication. Isn't that something you kick yourself for not having thought of first? All of the flavors that girls love: Barbecue, peppermint, hot spice, Chocolatini, you name it. This way women can *also* enjoy the process. Tropical Breeze for the ethnics!

"My favorite all-time invention is called the Insuck-Ta-Side. I thought of this when I was killing a praying mantis at Mam-Mam's. All girls are afraid of insects. That's just a damn fact. You can't argue with that. I don't care how PC you are. So this is basically a vacuum with a long, thin hose that you aim at ceilings or corners. It'll suck up *anything* you want! But here's the best part: Flip a switch and the insect comes flying out. *They don't have to die.* It's clean yet efficient. Girls will love it. And I *love* girls! Specially if they're clean and efficient, *ha!*"

Randy's comfort dog for the evening, Benedict, begins to howl. The entire strip club seems to turn and look. Randy gives a proud wave and pops into his mouth a Pepperidge Farm Pumpkin Cheesecake Soft Dessert Cookie.

"Figured I'd give Benedict another chance," he explains, through his lusty chewing. "Told Harriet I was bringing the dog to an old age home. That's a lie, of course. But I'm serious this time: Really gotta wash the smell out of ol' Ben when I get him home. Can't forget this time. Bought more effective dandruff shampoo. *Stronger.* No flakes gonna be on this helpful little doggy. From the dollar store. *Off brand.* From China. God knows what the hell is in it, but god also knows that this is gonna work! *China* strong! They're gonna take over one day. Gotta learn their language.

"Was also hoping for free turkey sandwiches tonight. Didn't work." Randy laughs very hard. "Meanwhile, the owners here think I'm crazy! They think I have a *brain* condition! That's what I told them! And that's why I keep bringing the dog! *Wh-wh-wh-wha-whoopsy*!"

Randy stands and acts as if he's unsteady on his feet and has a brain condition. Around and around he limps. It is extraordinarily funny. One of the men sitting next the stage looks up and smiles, and then turns his attention back to the stripper shaking a plastic bow and arrow.

Randy steadies himself and continues over to the VIP section. His wallet is extended: a most generous peace offering on this most American of holidays …

Benedict barks happily. Randy drops another piece of turkey sandwich on the ground for him to *gobble gobble.*

"Hello there!" Randy says to the stripper dressed as a Native-American. "Hello there, Injun!"

"Hello, Randy!" she says, most happily.

"My *wampum* is a most generous offering to this pretty Injun! Randy like Indian's outfit *this* much."

Randy extends his arms wide. Benedict is pulled closer to Randy by way of his very tight leash.

Surely Benedict does not mind.

"Thanks!" exclaims the stripper. She shakes her plastic peace pipe, which looks very similar to a ceramic bong.

"I have here with my some special wampum," Randy says. "I hand over this most special wampum as a generous offering to this pretty, primitive Injun!"

"It's $5, you know that."

"Wampum is Indian money."

"I'm aware of that."

"Doth thee accept it, squaw?"

"Sure."

"What is your name, squaw?"

"Tonight? Or in real life?" she asks.

"Tonight, squaw. Thee already knows your name in real life."

"Becki."

Randy looks disappointed. Leaning way from the stripper, he whispers: "See, that's why I don't get along with most girls. I thought she'd say something funny, like Pee for Money. Or She Who Like to Watch Bulls Fuck. No. This one has a very poor sense of humor. I love her but she does. Fact. Most women do. Their humor IQ tends to be in the rumdum range. A lot of studies have proven this. I've read about it in *Maxim* magazine."

"Come on," says Becki the stripper. She appears to be enjoying Randy's company very much. "We have five minutes."

"And *how*!" Randy declares. And then to the men sitting around the rickety stage: "*Becki give good gum job for such tiny squaw!*"

The men smile.

There is so very much to be grateful for!

"I guess I'm a little sad at times," says Randy, "but then something like this happens and it just all makes it worthwhile. So it's not all bad."

The entire world should be most thankful for Randy S._____!

By way of a special lasso, Randy is lead over to the VIP area. Along the way, he "mistakenly" drops one copy of the latest issue of the *Potomac Almanac*—with himself on the cover—on the stage where the latest dancer gyrates. It's already signed.

What a *perfect* way to spend this most American of holidays!

An Outsider's Perspective!

DJ Carl the Great: "Wait a second. Let me finish this one thing. Okay. This is a good turnout, right? Not bad for a Thanksgiving. One song and then I have to get back. Big night. What do you want to know? About Randy? Are you shitting me? How did that come about? Jesus! Okay, so I'm Carl H._____, the DJ here, otherwise known as Carl the Great. Well, I got a few memories of Randy. I think everyone in this place must. Did Randy tell you about how he's made money by selling fake synthetic urine to firefighters in Somerset County? How he mixed up some Gatorade with a drop of lemon juice and sold it for real? Randy is still hiding from those guys and they are *big*, they are juiced from the roids! What else? Oh, he hates that movie *Wonder*. Says the people in it are too ugly. Not the kid, necessarily, but Owen Wilson. He believes in Big Foot. But he's convinced Big Foot is a Muslim. Randy once tried to hire a crisis actor instead of attending his cousin's funeral. That didn't work. One of the strippers told me he likes to play an Amish person: 'Riding a Buggy to the Market' or something like that. He loves 'We Built This City,' which is impossible for the girls to dance to. He wants to build a water park on what's left of his property. He's going to call it Ragin Effin' Insanity. There won't be any lifeguards because he hates them! Just rescue dogs. And a swim-up wave-pool bar, which could be logistically tough. I imagine a lot of drinks are going to get spilled. He's usually here for the holidays. Can I tell you about me? I'm the one with all the stories, man! I got enough patter to make your insides splatter. I'm mellow as a Jell-O. Slap my wrist and call me butterfingers. Okay, I have to put on a new song for the girls. Ain't a proper Thanksgiving without 2 Live Crew's 'Me So Horny'. And here we go now …"

Randy Facts!
Randy once ran into George Michael of the
Sports Machine but was too shy to say hi!

PLACES HE'D MOST LIKE TO DIE

At the head of a conga line in the Mexican section
of EPCOT Center

Nude, on a trampoline

"In the middle of one of those trust-game exercises. People
would go insane!"

"In my panic room with no one finding me for years!"

At the Superbowl, on the Jumbo Tron, giving the thumb's up.

In the "VIP Box" at a Truck and Tractor Pull

"In a dunk-'em-booth, taunting the people walking by!"

On the high-dive at the local pool

Ikea cafeteria, face-first in a heaping bowl of Swedish meatballs

In the mud pit at the Annapolis Renaissance Faire

While playing donkey basketball and winning

"My elbows on the rail of a Mississippi riverboat casino, with me
pondering all my crazy-ass-shit past adventures!"

Sandals Resort, Bahamas, strapped into a rented parasail

"In a vibrating massage chair at The Sharper Image!"

Riding the Tilt-a-Whirl at a church carnival as 'Funky Cold Medina' blasts over the loudspeakers.

At a Rock and Roll Fantasy Camp, stage diving

At a Civil War re-enactment, dressed as a private, leading the charge

At the Outback Restaurant, holding the "I Can't Believe I Just Ate 25 Racks of Ribs, Mate!" trophy

In a sweaty post-concert huddle with the Spin Doctors

In line for a funnel cake

Williamsburg, Virginia: Tri-corner hat, head in the stocks, kids taking pictures

"Back room of a Spencer's Gifts, next to the cock candles!"

Inside a Winnebago, Wal-Mart parking lot, Frederick, Maryland

On the toilet juggling

On the toilet playing the stock market

"On the toilet writing a fan note to Gillian Jacobs. Can you imagine how fucking impressed she'd be?!"

Chapter Seven:
TELLING IT LIKE IT IS!

"I ain't going to sit around and feel sorry for myself," says Randy, confidently. "If Nora wants to be president, let her. Whatever. I no longer even care. She'll go insane. There's too much responsibility. I feel sorry for her. Already heard she's suffering. Just too much craziness. That job ages anyone. Not me. But her. She looks terrible. And you know what? I feel totally free for the first time in years. That's mature of me to say but it's true."

Randy is sitting in Nora's house for the neighborhood association meeting. For the first time in the development's history, a meeting is *not* taking place within Randy's gorgeous $1.5 million dollar town home.

"It's a tragedy in a sense," says Randy, chewing on a mini hot dog *hors d'oeuvre*s. "It's like Ripken playing 2,000 consecutive games or whatever he played for the O's. That's a record that will never be broken. Mine won't either. But like I said, Nora's gonna go insane. Just too much for the normal person to handle. I ain't normal. That's why I could handle it."

"And the meeting shall come to order," announces Nora, from her ostentatious leather couch. "First order of business—"

"To suck my ass," Randy mumbles.

There is little laughter. Randy's constituents are deep in enemy territory and out of their "fun element."

"First order of business," Nora repeats, shooting Randy a glare that can only be described as hostile and negative. "The repaving of the entrance. Any thoughts on this?"

Arnold, aka Bam Bam, raises his hand. "I feel we should wait until after winter, as the salt and plow might just ruin what we fix."

"Idiot," mumbles Randy.

"That's a good point, Arnold," says Nora. "Perhaps we should wait. Any other thoughts on this?"

"I agree with Arnold," says Leigh C____.

"Course you do," mutters Randy. "Where's your wife? Still 'sick'?"

"Meaning what?" asks Leigh.

"Meaning you kiss major ass," says Randy, sadly. He didn't want to bring this up. But he has very little choice. It's just the truth. And Randy *always* tells the truth. He's genetically wired that way. "You're going to agree with the new president because that's what you *do*, Leigh. Like I never did anything for you."

"Besides giving me food poisoning with the half-off gutter crabs?"

"Those crabs were cheap. That is true, but they were also fresh. Or fresh enough," says Randy. "For being half off. And they didn't come from the gutter. They came from the Potomac. Or somewhere close."

"*Fresh enough*!" agrees the Dodger. "*Half off*!"

"I was in the hospital for two days," says Miss Y._____. "Thought I was going to damn near die. Wanted to anyway. Mary and Joseph, I was sick! I wanted to tell you at the last meeting, but was told not to stir the pot!"

"I *did* visit," says Randy with remarkable patience.

"For the Jamaican beef patties," says Natalie D._____. "Right? And then you left immediately. You were in my room for a minute."

"No, Natalie," says Randy good-naturedly. "That is not true. I only left after handing over to each of you a beautiful flower. To show my appreciation for your long and loyal service as my constituents. But, in retrospect, that was a major mistake. Look where it got me."

"*Mistake*!" screams the Dodger. "*Retrospeck*!"

"Flowers taken from my garden," says a muscular, bald-headed young man in a tight tank top. Another bald-headed man stands next to him.

"From your garden?" Randy asks, perplexed. "And you would know that *how?*"

The young man begins to answer but is refrained from doing so by his friend.

Perhaps they both feel intimidated by Randy's reputation for moral excellence, as well as an abundance of proof, as evidenced by a receipt that Randy is holding aloft?

"What are you holding?" asks the young man.

"And why should we care?" asks the other man.

"*This* would be the receipt for the flowers," says Randy. "So *that's* why I care."

"That could be *any* receipt," says the young man, accusingly. "From anywhere—"

"Just relax," says his friend, again making a hand movement, holding his friend back. *Not worth it,* the motion seems to say. *You cannot possibly win with somebody this honest and intelligent.*

"Anyway the crabs were perfect," says Randy. "And yes, they were half off. From a roadside stand. Crabber by the name of Happy. And he sells crabs. And his name is Happy. Because he makes people happy. With his half-off crabs."

"Sick as a dog," finishes Leigh. "Did you eat them?"

"I did not," says Randy.

"We were all sick," says Nora, from the couch. "But … perhaps that had nothing to do with the food that Randy served us."

"Exactly," says Randy. "*Thank you*, Nora. And I never eat half-off crabs. But that's just me."

"You're welcome, Randy," says Nora, slowly. "For now, we'll table the front entrance repaving." She refers to her Ipad. "Item number two—"

"Where's Mary Mary at?" asks Randy, concerned.

"She's a little under the weather," says Nora.

"And her hot ethnic nurse?"

"Probably watching Mary Mary," says Nora.

"Funny doormats," says Randy. "Let's talk funny doormats."

"Funny doormats," says Nora. "Yes. Funny doormats. Who here would like for each household to be forced to own at least one funny doormat to be placed before their main entryway?"

Randy right hand shoots high into the air. Roger Dodger's as well. They are a solid team.

"No one else?" asks Randy, a bit puzzled, glancing around. "You gotta be kidding me! *Incredible*!"

"Why waste our time on such matters?" asks the Australian banker.

"Here we go," says Randy. "*Kangaroo* court."

"Not everyone from Australia owns a kangaroo," says the Australian banker.

Randy makes an expression, as if to say, *Yeah, right.*

"I'd like to talk sidewalks," says Arnold. "Specifically how much it would take to fix the sidewalk in front of the bus stop on Seven Locks?"

"What's two times who gives a shit?" asks Randy.

"I really do feel we need to fix the sidewalk," says Arnold. "Before somebody gets themselves killed and we'd be liable."

"*Booooring*," says Randy, now lying flat on his back on the carpet, stretching his lithe slimness like a mountain lion taking his comfort.

The Dodger laughs. "*Boooooring*!" he repeats.

Randy plucks another mini hot dog from the serving tray. He grabs a few. *Why not?*

"Can we talk about landscaping?" asks Mrs. Y._____. "And why the company we hired only shows twice a month and not three times a month like they're supposed to?"

"Better idea," says Randy, sitting up. "Got a *better* idea."

"Here we go," says someone, it's not clear whom.

"RandyFest. Let's talk about *that*."

"Must we?" asks Leigh. "Last year's was a disaster."

"And how so?" Randy asks, genuinely intrigued. "A two day music fest and a ton of money earned is a *disaster*? Well, hey hey *hey*!" Randy makes a funny motion with his hands. "Then guess *what*? If that's the case, then I am one dancing *disaster*!"

Randy continues to shake his hands.

The Dodger screams with delight.

"*Disaster*! *Dancing*!"

"That may be the case," says Arnold, trying very hard not to laugh at Randy's funny hand movements, "but I'll tell you what I do *not* love. And that would be the smashed windows, the fires in backyards, the backed-up Port-A-Johns and all the rest of the bullshit we had to deal with."

Nora chimes in her with two cents: "Randy, that event did cause a lot of damage in the common grassy area."

And now the rest can only rudely pile on.

"No more outsiders coming into the development."

"The traffic was horrendous."

"The lead singer of the Aerosmith cover band ran nude through my basement. He was covered in jelly. Not petroleum. The *edible* kind."

Randy stops moving his hands in a funny manner.

"Dream On wasn't just a cover band," he says solemnly. "They also played their *own* material."

"Terrific," says Leigh.

"Then how about the Renaissance Festival?" Randy asks, encouragingly.

"A Renaissance Festival? In our common grassy area? Any reason why?" asks Arnold.

"You don't like watching two freaks wrestle in the mud?" asks Randy. "*I do.* Saucy wenches serving mead? You don't like *that*?"

"I'd have to say no, Randy."

It's Nora, of course.

"Then the petting zoo?" asks Randy, still positive. "I always loved that idea. That idea was *mine*."

"We did that last year. Did not work out. *At all*."

Again, Nora.

Randy responds: "I had no idea that the pastured bull would go on such a rampage."

He means it.

Randy stands and makes his way over to the leather couch. He's forever the diplomat, even in the face of such horrendous negativity. "May I?" he asks Nora, signaling that he'd like to take a seat next to her.

"If you must," says Nora, petulantly. "Actually, no. I'd rather you sit away from me."

Randy remains standing.

He's hurt.

It shows.

"I won't include what you've just said to me in my memoir. If you apologize. *Immediately*. And if you *also* apologize for your rudeness to my friend."

"The Dodger?" asks Arnold.

"No. To *him*," Randy says, pointing to the man standing to his right, taking notes.

"And that's another thing," says Nora. "Who is this guy? And why does he follow you everywhere? And why is he allowed here at our development meeting? Does he even live here?"

"*This guy*," explains Randy, "would be my memoirist. And yes, he lives in my guest room."

"*Memoirist?*" asks Nora. "What does that even mean?"

Slowly, as if to a child, Randy responds, "My *biographer*. I will give you one more chance. Apologize. Or ye shall appear in my book as you thusly appear in thee *actual* life."

"I'll take that chance," says Nora.

"*Chance!*" screams the Dodger.

"No, Dodger," says Randy. "You emphasize what *I* say."

"*I say!*" screams the Dodger. "*Emphasize!*"

"There we go," says Randy, proudly.

"*Go!*" emphasizes the Dodger. "*You say!*"

"Randy," continues Nora, not sounding very much like a leader, "you can either sit with the rest of the group or you can leave. That's just the way it is, okay?"

Nora seems to be cracking under the weight of this new leadership position. Randy was correct. It is *not* a good fit.

Randy, as always, remains perfectly calm. Turning to Bam Bam, he asks, "How's that new garage working out?"

"Great," says Arnold, aka Bam Bam.

"And your fence?" Randy asks Leigh. "How's that working out for you?"

"Fine," says Leigh.

"Thought so," says Randy. "Truly did."

"Randy," says Nora. "You invented the rules and then invented ways to *circumvent* those rules. For your *own* benefit. That won't be happening on *my* watch."

"You know what else won't be happening on your watch, Nora?" Randy asks, waiting for an answer he knows will never arrive.

"Yes?" she finally answers. "What?"

"*Fun,*" says Randy, shaking his head sadly. "No more *fun.* And that makes me *sad.*"

"I'm so sorry," says Nora.

"And you know what else?" Randy asks. "I don't got no time for this *shit.* Gotta *fuck ton* to accomplish."

"*Accomplish!*" echoes Roger Dodger. "*Fuck ton!*"

Nora looks frantic.

"Randy, there really is no need to leave. As an association, there surely must be ways for us to all come to a common agreement for the betterment of this development, not just for you but for all of us—"

"Agree on *this*," says Randy calmly and diplomatically, middle finger of his right hand extended. "Fuck *this*."

"*This*!" says the Dodger, also standing. "*Fuck*!"

"Lovely," says Nora.

"*Lovely*!" says the Dodger.

"Let him go," says a person whose first name may not be mentioned for legal reasons. She sued to make sure of that. "Just let him go, like the wild animal he is."

If Randy has heard this outrageous, cowardly statement, the great man refuses to let on.

"See ya on the rebound," he responds diplomatically. With his dignity held as high as his middle finger still extended, Randy smoothly exits the house.

Meanwhile, loyal pal Roger is right by his side, a middle finger also extended, albeit straight down.

"Fucking idiots," says Randy once outside and free. "I *promise* you, Roger. I promise you on Mam-Mam's grave, which is buried right here on this property and which the authorities will *never, ever* find, because it's illegally buried under someone's house without them knowing about it: I swear to you that one day, and one day soon enough, these assholes will be practically *begging* me to return as president!"

"*Soon enough*! *Fucking idiots*! *Begging*!"

"C'mon, idiot," says Randy, super affectionately. "There's no time to waste. Time to *television*."

Randy puts his arm around the Dodger's shoulder. But there's a look of exhaustion on the great man's face.

Even the best of men can succumb to what Randy's favorite superhero once uttered for all the world to hear: "With great power comes great responsibility."

Randy and the Dodger walk towards Randy's $1.5 million town home. They disappear over the horizon, backlit by a gorgeous sunset, two heroes pounding the pavement so selflessly only for the betterment of all of humanity.

The Dodger goes to high-five Randy.

Randy continues on, a man alone, too burdened by his own pressing demands to respond to the request.

The high-five goes unanswered.

As it sometimes must.

Randy Facts!
Randy has never eaten a plantain!

FUN THINGS TO DO WHILE NUDE

"Fill out tax forms."

"Call the I.R.S. and complain about stuff."

"Order a Dunkin' Donuts coffee in the Drive Thru line.
The car can be a rental."

"Trampoline in a neighbor's yard."

"Drive past a high school and wave."

"Play the slide whistle in a tree outside someone's window.
You don't have to even know them."

"Make prank phone calls to suicide hotlines."

Chapter Eight:
AN EPIPHANY!

"*Randy*! You are *live* on Sports Addicts!" says the voice from Randy's living room stereo.

It's 9:30 A.M. and Randy is already up and about. He's still a bit tipsy from last night's mint Schnapps orgy, now well into its fifteenth straight hour.

"Long time no hear!" announces Billy "Punch" Foster, one of the show's four hilarious, long-time hosts. "Where you been at, son?"

"Yeah! Hell you been hiding?" asks Eric "Kimo" Kimmelson. "You calling from the Rockville Detention Center?"

The four hosts laugh. Randy can't help but laugh, too.

"Randy had *one* call to make from prison and he calls *us*," says Terrance Jason "T.J." Butler. "*I* wouldn't even call us!"

More laughter. Again, it's difficult for Randy not to join in.

"What were you arrested for *that* time?" asks Punch. "Taking a dump behind another old age home?"

"Or in a booth inside a Bob's Big Boy?" chimes in Kimo. "Now there's a *daily special*!"

"Or were you *doo-wah-diddying* in the handicapped stall at a Dave & Buster's?!" asks T.J. "Dandy Randy is *always* on a tear!"

"A *brown* tear!" finishes Kimo.

As with all of his live radio appearances, Randy is taping this broadcast on a cassette for posterity. He keeps all of his cassettes within a special fire-proof safe. He came upon this idea while watching a documentary on Scientology, a religion he greatly admires for its devotion to preserving the holy words of its late leader. And while Randy's fire-proof safe is not necessarily "nuclear bomb attack proof," he does feel confident enough in the fact that his words will be sure to last "three, four generations."

"Nah," says Randy, all casual. "Just wanted to call. Feeling a little low."

"How about falling asleep on top of your Hummer at a stop light? That happen again recently?" asks Punch.

"In front of a damn elementary school!" adds Kimo. "Imagine how that looked to the parents!"

The boys explode in laughter.

Over the next twenty-one minutes, until the Addicts shoot over to a commercial for Tyson's Rain Forest Cafe, Randy digs deep and holds absolutely nothing back.

Randy talks of the presidential coup within his development. He talks of how he and April are not always on the same intellectual wavelength. He talks about how he recently learned that his copyright application for the 18-shooter cereal dispenser—The Cereal Killah—had been denied; seems that an inventor in Ohio got to it first. He talks of how much he misses Mam-Mam, more so than ever around the holidays. He thought about her recently when he threw out her favorite shag rug toilet cover because of the tremendous mold and odor.

"Wait? Is this the same Mam-Mam who paid for your break-dancing lessons when you were twenty-one?" asks Kimo. The rest of the gang laugh. Each is right there with Randy, boosting his spirits, just good friends, shooting the breeze, showing that they're all in this crazy thing called life together.

Now the rest of the group provides their own delightful Mam-Mam memories:

"Is this the same Mam-Mam who paid for your Navy SEAL training camp in the backyard when you were twenty-five?"

"The same Mam-Mam whose diabetic socks you were forced to buy in bulk at the dollar store?"

"Is this the same Mam-Mam who'd pick up the phone and scream at the Addicts when you were live on the air?"

"WHO IS THIS?! WHAT ARE YOU SAYING ABOUT MY RANDY?!" imitates T.J. "BE NICE! BE KIND!"

"Ha ha," laughs Randy, enjoying the camaraderie. "Tee hee hee."

"Hey, Randy! Did you hear?" asks Kimo. "I saw your invention that sucks up bugs! I saw it on TV. I kid you not: Bugs Bee Gone. On Shark Tank."

"Really?" asks Randy, taken aback. "Are you kidding?"

"I'm not kidding," says Kimo. "Sorry, dude! Looks like your idea for the In-Sick-Dude-Size, or whatever the hell it's called, wasn't the first. Seems like a habit of yours! Remember your toy idea where you could pop fake zits? That's out now! Looks like you have a bit of a track record with all this!"

"Oh," says Randy. "That's ... wow. *Hoo* boy! Damn. That's ... oooh boy. Jerks always stealing my ideas. *Frustrating.*"

"WHO IS THIS?!" T.J. cuts in. "WHAT ARE YOU SAYING ABOUT MY RANDY?! BE NICE! BE KIND!"

An explosion of laughter.

"Hey, Randy. Been fired from any temp jobs recently?!"

"I forgot all about that!" yells Punch. "Randy shutting down the entire computer network at the World Bank?! THE WORLD BANK?! *Uh-oh!!!!*"

"Didn't the Feds get involved?" asks Kimo.

Randy, sensing it might be a good time to change the topic because of ongoing litigation with the World Bank, tells his on-air friends that he's really looking forward to coming alive this summer at his favorite place in the entire world ... "floating on a raft at Club Seacrets, gripping and ripping a Whiskey Shandy, a bevvy of hot-ass Bettys waiting impatiently on the bay's sandy shore. Club Seacrets ain't nicknamed Jamaica USA for nothin'! Oh, can you imagine?!"

There is much laughter and then the inevitable grilling of Randy being arrested a few times while in Ocean City for public displays of "in-DICK-na-cy."

And yet, as with before, it's all done in good, familial fun. And then the show's engineer plays a recorded tape of an NBA final buzzer.

Randy's line suddenly clicks off.

Just like that, he is no longer on the air.

Despite the desperate attempt by the Addicts to lift Randy's spirits, and despite the relief Randy feels after having talked to some really good friends about some very personal issues, Randy still looks a bit down. When told that it's very seldom he appears this sad, Randy nods. He can't help but agree.

"I've prayed on it," Randy says. "That's what Mam-Mam would do whenever she felt down. She was religious. *Jesus Christ Superstar* was her favorite movie. When I prayed last night, I had an epiphany. Do you know what an epiphany is? It's when something becomes clear when it wasn't clear before. And—"

Randy slurs the last "and," gives a quick gag, and falls asleep.

There will be no epiphany this morning.

Randy Facts!
Randy's favorite color is teal!

WEBSITE LOCATIONS RANDY IS CURRENTLY CYBERSQUATTING

americanredcriss.com

americangurldolll.com

marthastewert.com

newyorktims.com

okaycupid.net

okaycupid.gov

american-canther-society.com

montgomerycountymerryland.sex

harryteens.com

[Still waiting on the right price to sell. If you're interested, please get in touch with Randy at his email address: Numberonelover453@yahoo.com!!!]

Chapter Nine:
HORNDOG DAY!

"And ... *action*!"

Randy is sitting in his Ikea director's chair. Written on the back, across the canvas in black marker, is "RANDY – DIRECTOR!" It would be extremely easy to confuse this chair with any to be found on the biggest of Hollywood blockbuster movie sets.

The movie being made today is *Horndog Day.*

As promised, Randy's project is, indeed, getting made. With Randy directing. And writing. And producing.

Randy doesn't lie.

As he previously stated, Randy has always wanted to write, produce and direct a porn parody.

And now it's *happening.*

Randy does not stew within his own sadness juices.

"I want to see more feeling! *Really* play it up," declares Randy, in full director mode. "Really go *big*. You're a dude who gets laid every goddamn day but in a *different* way. Every freakin' morning your radio-alarm wakes you to Digital Underground's 'The Humpty Dance.' It's *hilarious*. And sexy. When you awake I want you to give a big ol' yawn and then look down at your crotch. You're popping a bootleg boner. Uh oh! Here we go ..."

The actor is a forty-something named Anthony W._____, famous in the Maryland area for his impressive work on the local dinner-theater circuit. His past roles include "Anti-Semitic Cossack" from *Fiddler on the Roof* and "Second Juggler" from *Barnum*, both at Toby's Dinner Theater in Olney. As a full-time gig, Tony works as a senior analyst at the IRRC, the Investor Responsibility Research

Center, in Dupont Circle. He evaluates institutional proxy reports. Randy found Tony on TaskRabbit under "Actors."

"Rub your eyes. You're exhausted. *'Oh no, I have to fuck all day again?!'* It's a burden. A burden I can *understand*," Randy giggles.

We're in the back room of the Baskin-Robbins Ice Cream in Cabin John Mall. Typically, this very special space is used only for children's birthday parties, but today it has been transformed—almost magically—into the absolute *perfect* location for a porn parody shoot.

"I was going to shoot at my own home, but the insurance costs are way too fucking prohibitive. This way, if something happens, Baskin-Robbins is responsible. I paid the manager to come down with a really bad case of 'I had no idea!' *'Hey! Did you know that they were shooting a porno in your birthday room!' 'I had NO idea! I thought it was just a birthday party for a naked guy!'* I'm paying a bundle. In cash. Whatever. The lighting is perfect. And the free ice cream don't hurt!"

The crew today consists of Randy using his iPhone as a camera. The set has a very professional feel.

"Anthony, you have a smear of Rocky Road on both bottom cheeks, let's clean that," Randy barks to his actor, then calls for a five minute break as Anthony wipes down his behind with a single Wet Nap.

After this showbiz task is completed (clearly, Anthony has done this before), Randy bellows through cupped hands made to resemble a temporary bullhorn: "Okay! Let's really *feel* this one!"

Randy presses the play button on his portable CD player, and the deep, rich sounds of "Humpty Dance" spring forth. "Tony, you're just waking up. *'Oh no, not again! Another day of scrumping?! Ah, I can't bear it!'* And ... *action*!"

"Ugh! I'm so tired! Not again! I have to fuck all day. I don't know how many more days I can take this!" exerts Anthony, in character as Phil Cummers, horny meteorologist. "My penis is so sore from fucking all day. Maybe I will try a new location for fucking? Perhaps in the town square?"

"Good," says Randy. "That was … good. But let's take it again. This time even more accentuated. *Really* sell it. And … *action*!"

Randy presses the play button on his portable CD player. "Humpty Dance" again starts. This is Anthony's cue to begin the scene. He sits up from the rented cot and rubs the sleep out of his eyes. "Ugh! I can't believe how tired I am! I have to fuck all day! No! Not again! I'm so tired of fucking! My penis hurts! It hurts from fucking all day!"

"And … cut! *Per-fuck-tion*!" declares Randy. "I *loved* that one! Nailed it. Ha *ha*! Now let's set up for the next scene. Where in the hell is Jenni?"

Jenni, an actress in the role of "Andie MacSwallow," is working late this afternoon at her shift at Michaels Arts and Crafts. Sadly, she isn't due to arrive for another fifteen minutes. Jenni's boss, store manager Chad, is unfairly making her re-organize the Wonder Foam display.

Randy peeks his head out the door of the party room and looks onto the main floor of the Baskin-Robbins. He calls: "Susan! Susan! You here?"

A teenager in a pink and brown uniform turns around, midway through dipping her ice cream scoop into a trough of murky water. "Um, yeah?"

"Could use some more ice cream, thank you," Randy states, no nonsense. "Make it a color that don't stain. Vanilla or something? And I'm out of wet naps! Got nothing to clean his bottom with anymore! And, hey! Do you want to be in a movie?"

"I don't … I don't think that's such a great idea, Randy," says Anthony from behind, still on the rented cot.

"Why?"

"She's … not legal. And she works here."

Randy nods. "Fine." Maybe Tony has a point. "Okay, Susan. Another time perhaps."

And then, back to Anthony: "Anthony, my boy, let's prepare for the money scene. Go wash your penis."

Anthony lifts himself off the rented cot.

"Jesus, man! Put on a bathrobe," says Randy, laughing very hard. "There are kids out *there*! C'mon! Head's *up*!"

"Your script is so fucking great," replies Anthony, also now laughing, "that I almost forgot I wasn't really visiting Cunts-a-Wanney!"

Anthony slips into a cotton *Rockville Marriott Courtyard* bathrobe and makes his way to the bathroom to wash his penis. He steps gingerly around a few children pointing to what ice cream flavors they want. Half way, Anthony pauses, as if someone's asked for his autograph, but continues when it's apparent that no one has.

"I have to get back to the script," Randy says, still in the back room, pointing to his 200-page, hand-written text. "You'll have to excuse me. The next scene takes place in the town square. There is no town square, so we're going to have to sneak onto the campus of N.I.H.", the National Institutes of Health, "and pretend that's where it's happening. As a tax payer, I help pay for that stupid place anyway. God, this is going to be good. So, so goddamn *good*."

The script is, indeed, very special. But this is not Randy's only script. Not even close.

Over the years, Randy has written more than seventeen porn-spoof scripts, although (until today) none has yet to be produced. Some of these include: *Schindler's Tryst, 12 Years a Knave, Guardians of Alex C., The Squirt Locker, The Fast and the Hairless, Meaty Balls, A Star is Horn-Y,* and *The Zodiac Driller.*

In addition, Randy has written a porn-spoof of *E.T.*

It's called *B.M.*

A gassy alien is unable to refrain from eating "aerosol can

cheese." The alien also loves to fuck.

But it's *Horndog Day* that comes closest to Randy's heart. There's just something about a guy waking up every day in order to make love over and over that tickles Randy's funny "bone."

"Mommy! Mommy!" cries a little girl, barging her way into the back room. "Look! *Look*! A movie! A *movie*!"

"Come back, honey," declares the mother, grabbing her daughter forcefully by her overalls. There is a sense of panic in her voice. "Back this way, baby! Back to the ice cream! *This* way, honey!"

Randy isn't listening. He's now wiping down the 12-inch black dildo that's needed for the next scene.

No detail is too slight to ignore.

And it seems that nothing—not even a curious child or an 18-year-old actress late from her afternoon shift at Michaels—is going to stand in this auteur's way.

"Back this way, baby!" screams the mother. "Please! Back to the ice cream! *This* way, honey! Honey! Honey! *Honey*? …"

Randy Facts!
Randy's favorite *Alf* episode
is the one where Alf
joins the Marines!

SOME OF RANDY'S
UNDERRATED THINGS

Taking a shit while wearing a fancy top hat

That podcast about salty snacks

Getting fuzzy on mojitos (powdered kind you can get
at The Giant)

The game "fuck, fight, or tickle"

The PopPerks at Doc Popcorns

Women's underarms (they're like something you're not allowed to
see but *are* allowed to see. It's pretty awesome.)

Funny jokes and things

Listening to the Sports Addicts while hot-tubbing

My "fellatio kit"

Frickles

Sitting on the hill across from the Pooks Hill Marriott, watching
the prom dates arrive in their rented limos

Getting high and playing digital foosball

Fantasizing about having an alien pet

My framed diploma from drunk driving school

The satin crew jacket from my all-time favorite Holocaust movie
Life is Beautiful that I once bought off ebay for $14

Hot ethnic nurses from the islands

Tanning booth prices in August

Subletting Ocean City Airbnbs

The garlic knots at the Watering Hole

Lazy Friday mornings in bed

The Hand Jive scene from *Grease*

Going shirtless on an airport jitney

Lt. Dan's Hot Beef Bites

The entire "Life Goes On" series on DVD, with a special
commentary track from Chris Burke and Chad Lowe

The Homer Simpson cookie jar that "defecates" Oreos

My autographed photo from one of the elves in *Elf*

The art of Thomas Kinkade

Puss

Chapter Ten:
A LIVE READING!

Randy rolls his eyes. He's bored.

Randy is far from impressed with what he's been forced to listen to over these past forty-seven minutes at this writing workshop at the Bethesda Writer's Center.

The first to speak was a woman who wrote a poem about the return of her cancer. *Yawn.* Then there was a gentleman who wrote about his sexuality and his "coming out" at the age of fifty-three to his Mormon family. *Who cares?* Then there was the college-aged woman with a nose ring who penned a short story about the sexy vampire who was "addicted to snuggles." *Good one.* And then there was the weepy grandmother and her story about a blind granddaughter with Obsessive Compulsive Disorder. *Hoo boy!*

Randy is having none of it. He is itching to get up before the rest of the group to read from his own work. This is Randy's first time at the Center but he's hoping for the equivalent of literary lightning to strike: *Perhaps his teacher could be so kind as to provide him with the name of a literary agent in New York City?*

That is … *If the teacher is impressed enough with Randy's writings?*
To Randy, this is a done deal. *How could she not be?*

But first he has to wait for yet one more poet, a middle-aged woman, to finish her poem. It's about a television show called *Unlikely Animal Friends* and about how it's the *perfect* metaphor for *all* different human races to come together and unite as *one.*

At last—after the poet rhymes "terrapin" with "African-American"—she steps down and takes a seat. A smattering of applause. It's now Randy's turn. He strides to the podium as if he's been doing this for years.

In his head, he has been.

"Ahem," Randy declares, taking a sip of water. He's waiting for the audience of six to settle in for the ride of a lifetime.

"*Ahem*," Randy repeats, this time louder. And then officially: "My name is Randy S._____. I am a poet. I am an author, a songwriter, a screenwriter, a performer. An artist of this great ride we call life. And I have experienced a great, *great* deal!"

At this, Randy straightens his red T-shirt that features a Washington Redskin scalping a Dallas Cowboy. "This is a poem I wrote called 'Life.' I wrote it for an old flame. She didn't appreciate it. Maybe you will."

And off he flies:

> *"My penis ain't thick*
> *but it certainly does the trick …*
> *Is that really why you left me?*
> *Or was it because I spied on you from a tree?*
> *Looked right into your room to see you undress?*
> *God, that whole thing was a mess.*
>
> *Got the idea from* Back to the Future.
> *Bet you now wish you could have been way, way cooler.*
> *I apologized ten million times!*
> *And even once in rhyme!*
>
> *But that's okay. Your boy is now nearly famous,*
> *While you're in Hagerstown, married to an absolute mess.*
> *Guy has no job, no life, just a big fat zero!*
> *Bet he couldn't hold a torch to this one-of-a-kind hero.*

Dude went overseas for the Marines.
Sing me a sad song.
Randy's got legs. Does HE?"

With this, Randy waits for the applause. While still waiting, he says by way of explanation, "We had a thing for a few months. I was twenty. She left me for a Marine. *Great move*. I'm being sarcastic. Ha *ha*!"

Randy makes a funny face.

At this, the audience joins together in applause and laughter. "No, I'm serious," corrects Randy, interrupting. "This really happened."

The laughter dies down.

There are some murmurings. And confused enquiries.

Is this yet another instance—one of many—in which Randy is being unfairly misjudged and misunderstood by his "fellow citizens"? In which his artistic abilities are not adequately recognized and respected? Most likely, yes.

No matter. Life is too short to be stung by the occasional rejection. And Randy isn't stopping now. Far from it. He claps his hands together to regain the room's attention. What he's about to say is *exceedingly* important.

Randy spreads his powerful arms wide, as if to prove that he's offering a priceless gift. "That was just the warm up! I have something very exciting for you to witness! I do. I would like to now show you my latest movie. If you'll honor me, I'd like to think of this as my world premiere. You can think of it that way, too!"

The leader of the workshop, a professional writer by the name of Brenda Z._____, looks concerned. "How long is this movie, Randy? And what does any of this have to do with writing?"

"Thirty-five minutes and I wrote it. So *that's* what it has to do with writing."

Randy pulls out his 13-inch MacBook Air from his *Big Pecker's*

Bar & Grill Ocean City tote bag. He places the laptop on the table and makes a motion for someone, *anyone*, to turn off the lights. The homosexual Mormon does so.

Randy clicks the start button for the movie to begin, and Anthony W._____, playing the role of Phil Cummers, appears on the screen. He's nude, standing before a map of Maryland, holding a cordless microphone and talking to the camera as if he's a weatherman. "Today's forecast calls for horniness. There is a 25% chance of a powerful B-job ... and a 100% chance of an explosive sperm front!"

"Enjoy," says Randy, walking towards the door. "I'll be next door getting an everything bagel."

Once in the elevator, Randy states: "Gonna blow their minds. I'm like the gatekeeper. They need an excuse to break out of their confined creative lives. This is the key. I'm the dungeon master. You ever play D&D? I used to play by myself. That's a good metaphor for life. Be willing to take risks ...whether it's attacking a highly-charismatic wizard or showing your porn parody to a class of Mediocre Marys and Lame-Ass Larrys."

After exiting the Writer's Center, and after borrowing six quarters to plunk into the parking meter next to his Hummer, Randy strides a few doors down and into Bagel City.

Stepping confidently up to the counter, Randy asks, "Where's Samantha?"

"She's not in today," responds a teen worker wearing a Bagel City baseball cap.

"*Goddamnit!*" exclaims Randy. "She's the only one who knows how to make my bagel the way I *like* it. She *knows* me. She knows the way I *like* it. Damn it!"

"I can definitely try," suggests the young woman. "How would you *like* it?"

"Everything bagel, toasted *well*, with just a hint of regular cream cheese," replies Randy. "I hate it when it's all glopped on. No low-fat.

Regular. I fucking *despise* low-fat."

"I think I can do that," says the woman. "Will that be all?"

"You say 'that's all' like you've already accomplished it. Yes, *that's all*."

Randy, with a crisp, borrowed $5 bill, pays and, after accepting the $1.75 in change, makes his way past the tip jar and over to his favorite table, one facing the street. "I never face a wall when I eat," Randy explains. "Or look into a mirror when I shit. Why do people do that? Am I a goddamn monkey?

He sighs dramatically.

"I don't know. I guess I should be in a better mood. Yeah. I don't know. Everything with *Horndog Day* is finished and people can finally just enjoy it. It's all smooth sailing. Don't know why I'm so mad today."

Randy is referring to the fact that *Horndog Day* is "in the can," as Hollywood professionals might say. Randy has paid nearly all of his fines for illegally shooting on the grounds of the National Institutes of Health. The obligatory negative articles in the *Potomac Almanac* have come and gone. The mean-spirited letters from the Baskin-Robbins executives have been tossed. It's again time to think only of the unlimited future.

"You asked me earlier about my career arc. You interrupted me. I want to get more into that. I'm a scrapper. A hustler. I earned my B.S. on the streets. I don't have college experience beyond that one semester of communications at Montgomery College. I've worked from the time I was thirteen, delivering the *Potomac Almanac*. Ironic that they're now the publication after me the most. Then again, they're still mad at me for hoarding a year's worth of copies without delivering a single issue. But I'm glad I did that. I've never stopped working.

"When I was older, fifteen or so, I'd help Mam-Mam at the Hallmark store during summers. She'd pay me with cinnamon rolls. When she opened her lice salon, I was in charge of the paper towels and the comb cleaning. I still have three lice combs with my name on them in fancy cursive. My first *real* job was at sixteen. I worked the register at Pep Boys. From there, I kept working my way up. Worked a few years selling fake synthetic urine. Just Gatorade with a drop of lemon juice. That went fantastic. But I do have to keep a low profile from firemen. I hate them.

"Here's a funny work story. Was working on a moving crew when I was seventeen, eighteen. Actually, my first day on the job. It was fifteen miles away. Didn't have a kick-ass car then. Didn't have anything, so I had to walk. A cop pulls up. 'Where you going?' 'To work. I don't have a car. I have to walk.' 'How far?' 'Fifteen miles.' 'That's incredible! Let me drive you there! I admire your work ethic!' So the cop drives me there and tells the owner that I'm so dedicated I was willing to walk fifteen miles. The owner's mind is blown. Can't believe it. 'Here's what I'm gonna do! I'm gonna give you my car! I was looking to get a new one anyway! We need people like you to work here. I love your work ethic! I *love* it! Keep up the *great* work!'

"Quit the next day. Job sucked. That's how I got my first car.

"Where else did I work? Bus boy at C.J.s Pizza. Mulch guy at Hechinger's. Sales rep at Pen Boutique. Worked the floor at the Big Screen Store. Bank temp. Movie director. Small business owner. Have I told you about that? The Float & Smoke, the country's first waterbed store to sell vapes. Didn't work out for me. It was all too new. Ahead of its time. That was open for a month. Until the idiot lit himself on fire. Now in a cool wheelchair. With a new face. *That I paid for!* What I'm saying is that I've *more* than earned my right to ask for a bagel any *damn* way I please.

"Sometimes when I'm bored, like now, I'll just start *jelqing*. You know what *jelqing* means? That's a penis-stretching exercise I learned from my Indian friend. Not *ay-yi-yi-yi* Indian, but *Indian food* Indian. We're *amazing* Facebook friends. I'm going to start if you want to divert your eyes—

"Oh, here we go. Let's see if these idiots got it right."

A restaurant employee, different from the worker who had earlier taken Randy's order, walks over with a plastic tray and places it on the table. Randy says nothing, merely mouthing: *Wait. Right. Here.* He accentuates each of the three silent words by thrusting a forefinger skyward.

With the greatest of care, Randy checks over his bagel, meticulously pulling it apart. He then expertly holds up one half toward the light in order to inspect it even more carefully.

The man is a perfectionist … which is why he so despises *imperfection.*

"'Tis fine," Randy finally announces with a Shakespearean flourish. "I should say, *'Tis adequate.* Could have been better toasted with a *lot* less cream cheese. But I'm not going to be a *dick.* I'll just come back when Samantha's working. *Thank* you." He motions for the employee to exit.

She smiles and leaves.

"Don't get me wrong. Not everything I've been involved with over the years has been a huge success," Randy continues, between bites of his acceptably toasted bagel. "There was that pop-up trampoline store behind Wintergreen Mall. That would have been a huge success if not for those two morons who broke their necks. Which is kind of too bad. Did you know that *clitoris* is ancient Greek for 'the devil's raspberry'? That's true. I never forget anything. It's a burden. Sometimes I feel like my mind is exploding. Just too many goddamn thoughts. What I'm saying is that I've *earned* my place in society. But I can be picky. I can be *particular.*"

The woman to whom Randy gave his original order now approaches the table.

"Yes?" asks Randy.

"I've just come to see if the bagel is up to your exacting standards?" she asks.

"Good enough."

"Great," she says. "That makes me *extraordinarily* happy."

She walks away.

"Bitch was being sarcastic," says Randy, shaking his head sadly. "I can tell. Not everyone can. *All aboard the Choo Choo Female! Next stop ... Crazy Town!* That dame has a nasty case of defeatism. If you hang around that type long enough, you inherit a bad case of *attitude* sickness. Just a big load of applesauce. *Not going to happen to me.* Fuck it. Let's jet!"

Randy stands from the table and dramatically points to his barely-eaten bagel. The workers turn to look. His intention is clear. He is not happy. One has to wonder if these workers will one day experience great pangs of regret when they read about themselves acting as fools in a best-selling memoir.

This occurs to Randy, as well. Aloud, he asks: "Do all of you really want to be portrayed as losers in my book? *Truly?*"

No one answers. Perhaps they're too intimidated by Randy's awesome, larger than persona and life force. But Randy has little doubt that they will all undoubtedly feel very silly for having underestimated him.

Sooner rather than later.

In the meantime, a room full of film critics anxiously await Randy's return. There are sure to be a lot of questions. And Randy intends to patiently answer each and every one, at least until he grows bored. The day is young and there is still so much left to accomplish.

"C'mon. Let's head back to the Uglies. I cannot wait to see their effin' faces!"

[Note: Hey-ho! This is Randy. Not Noah. Like everyone else in the entire world, I have a bucket list. This means things I want to do before I die. I thought I'd tell you about what I wanted to do *before I die ... before* I died!! Okay, here they are!]

THINGS TO DO BEFORE HE DIES

Bust ass down the entire length of the Amazon on my
banana-yellow Skidoo.

Finish writing that unauthorized Charlie Sheen biography.
This is going to be big.

Make friends with a couple Hell's Angels. Maybe even get beaten in.

Finally catch up on the TiVoed Seth MacFarlane-hosted Oscars.

Swim with a dolphin and later eat it.

Hug Steve Doocey.

Fuck a pair of conjoined twins. They HAVE to be hot.

Watch that documentary about the idiot who climbs Mount Aetna
without ropes.

Myth bust that bullshit about cats being able to safely land
on their feet.

Eat an entire crock of Brunswick Stew and ride the Tilt-a-Whirl.

Hang-glide buck naked.

Take a trip to the Afghan/Pakistan border. Can't be as bad as they say.

Kiss the Blarney stone, but safely, with a dental dam.

Petition to get Jim Belushi a star in the Hollywood walk of fame already!

Go to Rock and Roll Fantasy Camp and jam my fucking ass off with the great Kenny Loggins.

Fuck in a cave.

Root through Kid Rock's garbage for all the cool shit he probably throws away.

Crank call Phil Collins.

Collect ninja throwing stars.

Get a hum-hum while floating in a hot air balloon.

Get a hum-hum at the entrance to IRS headquarters.

Just get a hum-hum

Chapter Eleven: RANDY'S R&R!

A few days later, Randy decides to take a much needed week off. He's terribly fatigued from all the stress.

More so, he is bored intellectually.

"Even the biggest and most powerful computers burn out," he says. "And I'm playing 3-D chess here, but with myself. I don't know how to play 1-D chess but I need to expand my horizons. I'm tired of idiots talking down to me. Plus, my dermatology results came back negative."

It's Spring Break. Just as he's done every Spring Break for the past twelve years, Randy is heading down to Ft. Myers to party his ass off. It's a tradition.

"I have more fun down in that damn town than I do anywhere else. I hate to travel. *Never* do it. Except into D.C. maybe. But I don't consider this travel. This is F-U-N. That spells *fun*. And it *is*. But it hasn't always been without its stink-ass wrinkles."

Randy is leaning back in his Spirit Air seat, wearing his blow-up neck pillow, munching on a smuggled packet of peanuts.

"Not allowed on the plane," he states sarcastically in a baby voice, holding up the packet. "*Could be too dangerous for the allergic. That's a conspiracy theory. There are so many! 9/11 was a conspiracy created by the news organizations to have something to talk about. That's clear. Charlie Sheen talks about this. Michelle Obama has a penis. That is true. I've seen photos and charts. Adam and Eve were both sent to Earth from outer space. Where in the hell *else* would they come from?

"President Kennedy shot himself. I know this for a fact. Princess

Diana was killed by Mexican mercenaries. That's true. I don't believe Elvis is alive or any of that shit. I believe he never existed. That it was a government creation to take people's minds off war. As for that plane no one's ever found, it's in Greenland. When was the last time anyone said anything good or bad about Greenland? They wanted the world's attention. So they forced it to land. Pathetic. I *hate* those people."

Randy settles in for the two-and-a-half-hour flight. He has his iPhone mixes and his *Uncle John's Bathroom Reading* books and his Word Scrambles to puzzle over. But for now, Randy is more than content to just talk about his astonishing Spring Break adventures.

"I first started going when I was twenty-two. I was at Montgomery College. I quit. The professors were idiots. Never really had the opportunity to party. One year, I said fuck it. This is when I was working as a temp in Rockville. God, I *hated* that job! Bunch of morons. Just Xeroxed and shit. World Bank. I told them all to fuck off and I quit, but not before I left them a little present. Probably still smelling it. Just behind the fridge. Just next to my other gifts.

"So I thought, *Where should I head now?* I read something in *Maxim* about Spring Break and Ft. Myers sounded real cool. I drove on down." He laughs. "I couldn't afford the fancy air travel like I can now!

"So I go down. No place to stay. I checked fliers on light poles. There was a house that was looking for more people to offset costs. I show up. It's a bunch of fraternity types from University of Georgia. That's fine. The house is huge. I party my ass off. I see a triple rainbow. Hooked up with a lot of Bettys. Incredible. Fly a kite for the first time. Played Frisbee for the first time. Flew a kite for the *second* time. Played drinking games but not alone for a change. Got a tan line on my penis from where the cock ring was. I'm still *amazing* Facebook friends with a lot of these people!"

Randy throws a peanut above his head, just beneath an air vent, and masculinely catches it with one hand. He then proficiently pops it into his mouth.

"We called it the Frog Cave. The house was green like a cave where a frog might live. I've been going back ever since. I'm now in charge of the house. *Der commandant! Yavul!* I rent for the week, others pay me. I've never had trouble finding enough kids."

Randy sneezes very dramatically.

"Ugh. Sorry about that. Right on your face. Mam-Mam used to call that an angel's kiss. Or maybe it was the devil's kiss? I can't remember. So *crazy* shit has happened at the Frog Cave. *Insane.* Anything goes. You know why? *Cause you're in Randy's world now!*

"Slept with practically an entire nerd sorority from Tulane in 2008. *Boob it and pube it!* I have that down in my Fuck Journal. That was easy as hair pie. God, I *love* it down there. 2010 was the worst year! I suffered a 'break.' I went bazookas. Came to believe that hermit crabs were talking to me. Ran along the beach at night until I was tackled by a lifeguard. This is another reason I hate those fuckers. Bunch of Macho Murphys. He was off duty. The crabs were telling me to light the boardwalk on fire. I did as they told me. There were people on the boardwalk laughing, throwing fudge and taffy and shit. They were pouring cotton candy on the fire to put it out. Big fucking joke. They can kiss my tightly-clenched *buttocks*.

"The next year was much better. Ironically, I ended up selling bootleg hermit crabs on the boardwalk and made a shit ton of money. Most of the crabs died. I sold them as young, but they were old. The kids couldn't have afforded the more expensive ones anyway. *Everybody* wins.

"That was the year I was accused of stealing the Frog Cave's 'Rash Cash.' That's the money—mostly change—used for suntan lotion, condoms, huge bottles of Kwell, things like that. I didn't steal it. I was *borrowing* the money to pay for a henna tattoo. It was a Chinese symbol for 'virtuous.' That was also the year I got that bad sex thing. My groin itched so bad it glowed in the dark. That's happened a few times. So maybe that wasn't a good year. And the henna symbol turned out to be Chinese for 'halitosis.' A Chinese guy who worked at a restaurant told me. He thought it was fucking hilarious. And he later put it online. So that was a big joke."

The stewardess, an attractive woman who looks to be in her early twenties, strolls past with the beverage cart. Randy winks.

Surprisingly, she does not return the wink. She appears very busy. Maybe later.

"It's fun to be around people who are younger. They don't have as many hang-ups. No kids to worry about. That's good. No second mortgages. No talk about office bullshit. Who cares about your office problems? I don't. No talk of divorce. Besides, I look young. Been micro-dosing testosterone. I think we have a really solid group this year. They have to send me photos and they have to pay in cash. I'm excited. A *great* looking bunch!"

A different stewardess arrives and asks Randy if everything is okay, did he push the HELP button? Randy replies that he didn't push the HELP button but perhaps, just maybe, if it might be okay, and only if it would be, could he possibly have her cell phone number? The stewardess smiles. There's a glint of interest in her sparkling blue eyes. She walks away. Maybe later.

"I do have to be careful, though," Randy states, adjusting his neck pillow. "A few years ago some college girls made trouble for me. Or their boyfriends did. I somehow convinced them I was a photographer for *Vice*. I was putting together a photo spread. I asked them to pose nude behind a Lido's. They were really into it. The problem was my disposable single-use camera. It didn't look 'professional' enough. So that was hard to talk my way out of. They chased me and I escaped. I still have the pictures in a special album."

Randy effortlessly unclasps his seatbelt. He's extremely adept with complicated mechanisms.

"Speaking of which, time for me to make myself young. I look much younger than thirty-four, but my teeth are yellow. I'll *admit* to that. Everyone in my family has yellow teeth. PopPop had yellow teeth until they fell out. Then he had yellow dentures. I could never understand that. That's why you buy fake white teeth! He was an idiot. So I bleach. And I wear a baseball cap backwards. I can easily pass for twenty-two, twenty-four at the most, especially with a ton of face lotion. I'll see you in a half hour."

Randy slaps on his Orioles baseball cap, twists it backwards, and slides into the aisle.

"I'm gonna look so goddamn sweet that gay guys will fucking want to sleep with me! I'm not gay. I've had *one* homosexual experience. I fucked a male deer. I should say that I *dreamed* I fucked a male deer. I love deer. We shook hands afterwards. I have no problem with gays. But here's the thing about me: I'm way, way more into the *rose* than the *hose*!"

With that, Randy heads on back to the lavatory. There's work that needs to be accomplished. It's Spring Break.

Before he does so, however, Randy gives a hearty wink to his attractive seatmate who, unexpectedly, doesn't seem to return his generous display of affection.

Maybe later.

For Randy and his friends at the Frog Cave, it's almost time for *one* thing:

F-U-N.

And that spells *fun*!

[Note: Hey! This is Randy. Not Noah. I love movies. I put together a list of my favorite 64. No order beyond they're all really fucking amazing!]

RANDY'S FAVORITE 64 MOVIES

White Chicks ("seen it a million times. Fucking hilarious!")

The Golden Child

Jack and Jill ("Adam Sandler always makes me laugh.")

Mr. Holland's Opus ("The kid was deaf but sweet")

Drive

Heaven is for Real ("it is. I've been there.")

Drillbit Taylor

Who Framed Roger Rabbit

Buster

Walk Like a Man ("Howie Mandel is raised by wolves
or something")

Last Tango in Paris ("you got to have the sound off")

Year One

Superbad ("I love anything Judd Apatow does!")

Judge Dredd ("Stallone only")

Zookeeper

The Sitter

Pirates of the Caribbean: On Stranger Tides

Cowboys and Aliens

Arthur ("The new one. I can't understand the European one.")

Norbit

Daddy Day Camp

The Number 23 ("This picture will blow your mind. 23 is now my favorite number.")

Napoleon Dynamite ("I know every line except for the romance stuff.")

Dodgeball

Nacho Libre

The Cobbler ("This movie made me cry. I told you I liked Adam Sandler!")

Ted 2

Entourage ("The fucking best")

Hook

Baby Geniuses ("the special effects are outrageous")

Universal Soldier: The Return

Chill Factor

Dream a Little Dream

Communion ("It's all true. God, I'd love to be picked up by aliens and taken to another planet. I'd be real popular. 'Would you want an anal exam?' 'Sure! Why not?!'")

The Karate Kid Part III ("the best of the bunch. Ralph Macchio was forty-seven when he shot this one")

The Adventures of Ford Fairlane

Dice Rules ("the most hilarious live stand-up concert ever caught on film")

Slappy and the Stinkers

I Still Don't Know What I Did Last Summer

A Night at the Roxbury ("this classic never shows up on any best-of lists but it's so fucking good. You can't ask for more in a comedy than this one.")

Chairman of the Board ("I laughed so hard I pissed into the lap of the guy sitting next to me. This was at home. Just joking. Not about the pissing.")

Rock Dog

Hardly Working

The Emoji Movie ("The critics blasted it but it's really subversively brilliant. I hate critics.")

Alice Through the Looking Glass ("trippy")

Zoolander 2 ("even funnier than 1")

Gods of Egypt

Dirty Grandpa ("when the fake grandpa takes a dump in an airport jitney I cried I laughed so hard")

Scary Movie 5

Life is Beautiful ("the best Holocaust movie ever made. I hate nudity in Holocaust films and this didn't have any which is good.")

Bucky Larson: Born to Be a Star ("Pauly Shore is the best. Where did he go?")

Atlas Shrugged III: Who is John Galt?

Nobody's Perfekt

Jesus Christ Superstar ("Mam-Mam's favorite. I love it except for the goofy hats on the soldiers. And the music.")

The Last Airbender

Faces of Death II ("real people dying years before the invention of the internet, incredible")

Carbon Copy ("Way ahead of its time when it comes to talking about race issues")

The Slugger's Wife

Fraternity Vacation

The Star Wars one about Han Solo. The best one of them all.

Summer Rental

Corky Romano

Black Knight

Scary Movie 2

The Three Stooges ("The new ones, not the dopey old ones")

"This is me at Best Buy. I don't smile when I shop. I ain't no whistlin' pimp. This is the store in Tyson's Corner. I like this one because it has a better selection of DVDs. I like to get there at 5:00 PM, after the kids leave and before the stupid-ass government workers come home from their 'work.' I once saw a homeless guy shoplifting a waffle maker. I'm not sure why. Noah took this shot. This was the same day I had diarrhea from eating too much fried rice that I bought at that place in Cabin John Mall. I haven't eaten there since."

"I have a ton of ideas for movies and children's books. Like a friendly unicorn really impresses a small town with its beauty and ability to make everyone laugh. But he has irritable bowel syndrome. He must be killed because he stinks like shit. That's funny. Another children's book idea would be a drummer boy in the Civil War who insists on playing a long solo on his roto-toms, like the ones Alex Van Halen plays in Van Halen. It goes on for thirty minutes. Other soldiers beg him to stop but he refuses. He's then shot in the head but it was worth it. This one would be serious. Excited."

"I took this myself. It's arty. That's me. I'm always thinking in terms of creativity. It kind of looks like I'm an angel. I saw an angel once. It was sitting at the bottom of my bed, reading. I went back to sleep. I don't know why people are so afraid of ghosts. All they do is knock shit off dressers. Would love to meet a hot ghost. I'd be real gentle with her. I'd then make her scare all the people I hate, like that manager at the Baskin-Robbins who refuses me more than five pink spoon samples. I would love to do that!"

"Me walking the C+O canal. I'm wearing the slacks I always wear out to bars and night-clubs. It still has a mustard stain on it that's impossible to get out. But these are super fucking comfy. I like to walk real fast. I'm not sure this photo captures just how fast I'm walking but it's super fast. That's not bragging. That's just the truth. Noah took this shot. He's not a very good photographer and he'd be the first to admit that. I once saw a dead owl lying next to the canal. Freaked the shit out of me. I wrote a poem about it."

"Just chillin'. I'm not a huge fan of history. I've never actually taken the time to read what any of these signs say. I have better things to do. I'm wearing a wedding ring because girls feel safer when they see that. This photo shows off my muscles pretty good. I like to micro-dose testosterone. That helps. I do twenty-five crunches a day. My crunch song is 'American Heartbeat' by Survivor."

"One of my favorite animals is the bald eagle. Another would be the armadillo. I would love to eat eagle but I heard the meat is super fucking tough. Like Americans. Maybe I'd just add some Old Bay. I love Old Bay. I even put it on my pancakes. This photo was shot near the Fuddruckers on 355. I love Fuddruckers but I hate to touch the mustard pumps. They should have automatic mustard dispensers like they have inside hospital bathrooms. That's a good idea. I might invent that."

This was taken in front of the Baskin-Robbins that I hate. It's next to a music store I sometimes go into to bang on all the drums until I'm asked to leave. That's not my bike. This is the Baskin-Robbins where the dipshit manager won't allow me more than five pink spoon samples. I need at least ten. Sometimes I'll just sit here and scowl. If you look real close, you can see the manager in the store. Knowing this asshole, he's probably telling off a kid. This is not the store where I shot the porn parody *Horndog Day*. That turned out well."

"In front of my development. This is the entrance I like to use. There are four. If you look real close, you can see that a golf cart is entering the development. I have no idea why but it's cool."

"I'm a huge fan of the Skins. Always have been. I don't understand all that bullshit about how it's not fair to Indians. But I can definitely understand if Indians are pissed that the Skins haven't won in years. I hate the Redskins owner. He has the balls to charge $15 for a beer but he can't fucking put together a winning team. He's only good at marketing. I emailed him once but he never got back to me. I had some suggestions. I don't mind a no. Would just love to have him write back like a man. I once met Joe Theismann at the bar he owns in Old Town. Nice guy. I took a photo with him but I lost it after we sold Mam-Mam's farm. I asked to see Joe's knee scar and he said no. That's cool. Probably brings back some not so cool memories."

"One of the greatest joys in my life is seeing how incredibly close my 24-year-old escort, April, has become with my hundreds of hermit crabs."

"I only drink IPA beers. Any other type is for amateurs. I love Instagram pages on beer. I love baseball. I used to play it all the time and I was good. I hate softball because only fat idiots and lesbians play it. I also hate soccer and tennis. Especially volleyball. One hit, two hit, three hits, then the point is over. Pathetic. Beach volleyball is cool enough, at least to watch. I love digital foosball. Nowadays I like to watch football all day on Sunday. I start at 11:00 and go until 11:00. I consider that a full NFL lap."

"This is my good Facebook friend Mike Mezzer. He's paying me $50 each time I put his photo into the book. He likes to take photos in front of the old Lorton prison. I don't know why. Strange guy. He's always wanted to be in a published book. I really fucking love this shot. He better fucking pay me!"

"This is my good Facebook friend Mike Mezzer again. I told him to pose in front of an Outback. He did. He goes here every Tuesday night. The people who work here know him. He once saw a midget eating a big rack of ribs which he found very funny. Mike works in auto repair in Arlington."

"This made me laugh like crazy. Mike Mezzer posted this on his Facebook page. He now owes me $150."

"You're not supposed to take selfies when you drive but I don't care. I think it really captures who I am. I was driving down Gainsborough Road in Potomac, just past Windsor View. I don't remember why but I wrote it down. I did let one rip and it later made my Fart Journal. I gave it a 4, which is pretty damn good. I'm real fucking particular."

"Here's one of me in front of my favorite Fudd's. They have the best and most comfortable bathrooms. *The cleanest*. Fudd's it out!"

"Fucker now owes me $200. A shot of where Mike Mezzer lives in the Worland development in Potomac. His crazy ex girlfriend Kia took this. They broke up because Mike wasn't into weird shit."

"Me in front of the Teeters close to home. It looks like a fish is sitting on my shoulder but that's just a trick of the camera. I like Teeters because it has my favorite cheap toothpaste and I know everyone who works there. They have a great collection of greeting cards but a lot have to do with death. What's with all the sob stuff? I bought a funny one for Mam-Mam when she had the 'heimers but she didn't get it. It said something like 'I Hope You Get Better Soon' and it had a drawing of a guy with one of those dog collars that dogs wear after surgery. It was very funny. I still have it."

"Me inside the Teeters. They have amazing free cheese samples. Sometimes I'll eat an entire meal just standing. I'm sweating like a raccoon here. Hot ass day. One of the workers Betsy got botulism from gas station nacho cheese. She now poops through a stoma, which is a hole in the abdomen. That really sucks. But she washes her hands well before work. Or at least she says! Uh oh!"

"Alley behind the town homes. You can't see my home, on purpose. That's all I need. Some nutter showing up to bother me. Sometimes I throw a tennis ball against the garage door until a neighbor tells me to please stop. The key word is *please*."

"Best fucking burger in all of Maryland. Habit Burger Grill, Gaithersburg. Next to pet store where I buy my hermit crab food."

"Make that $250, cockcheese!"

"Till the day I die, girls will remain a mystery."

"I love comedy"

"Not far from the American Girl Store where I get my best writing done."

"I once slept with a girl in this building. I forget her name. She smelled good."

"Me looking west toward Seven Locks Road. Just thinkin' about stuff and shit."

"I like to go for a lot of walks in the development. This is one route that I take. I call it the 'Scenic Route.' There's also the 'Fast Route,' 'The Commercial Route,' 'The Long Route,' 'The Short Route,' as well as the 'Night Route,' the 'Day Route,' and the 'Round-a-Bout-and-Headed-Back-2-Nowhere Route.'"

"After a walk I like to sit and contemplate. Wave hi to people I know. Smoke a fat ass strawberry White Owl. I call it Sucking on Satan's Stick. I like to think about how much I'd hate to ever be locked up in a prison. Everyone's hole's a goal in jail. If you look close enough, you might just be able to make out a funny flag on the house behind me. It's a Redskin giving the finger. It's incredibly fucking funny."

"Sorry, but this is bad ass."

"Yeah. Right."

"I thought this would be an appropriate photo to put in last because it says STOP. I wish you could see it in color, it's amazing. Thanks again for reading. Whenever you drive around Maryland, think of me. That'd be cool."

Chapter Twelve:
BACK TO WORK!

"M. Night Shyamalan is a genius," proclaims Randy, walking at a very brisk and healthy pace along the C+O Canal path, just outside Seneca, Maryland. Randy does this at least once a week, for both the fresh air and for the exercise. Randy doesn't believe in gyms. They're "scams."

It's Spring in Maryland at last. There's a bounce to Randy's already mammoth step.

Randy is wearing a pair of orange Under Armour HeatGear Training shorts and a Washington Capitals tank top. On his feet are his preferred pair of walking shoes: unlaced yellow Converse Voltages, purchased from an online Japanese seller of vintage sneakers. In order to avoid paying the Maryland state tax, Randy shrewdly has most of his special packages—including illegal Mexican fireworks—sent to his P.O. Box at a Staples in Alexandria, Virginia.

The air is thick. Cicadas buzz from the fecund shores of the Potomac. The early spring heat and *hssssssing* don't at all lessen Randy's ability to expound on any topic. He's just returned home early from Spring Break at the Frog Cave.

"Wasn't a good fit this year. Very disappointing. Typically I'll hook up with a few Bettys. Only *one* this time. A freak with a Tweety Bird tattoo just above her nest. So that sucked. Her name was Natalie. *Natz.* And she said to me, 'Are you a diwty little kitty cat?' And I said, 'I'm not sure, why?' And she said, 'Tweety all *afwaid* of kitty cats.' That was a very long night. Dirty little soomka."

Randy pauses and looks toward the water.

"So there was a … situation this year. More like a snafu. That means 'situation normal, all fudged up.' I invited a homeless dude into the Frog Cave. Nice guy named Benjy. Super sweet. Not one of those homeless with an attitude. Just a dude a bit down on his luck. I felt bad for him. He was sleeping in front of the Bojangle's where I would always get my morning biscuits. I asked him to come back to the Cave and sleep on the couch. At first, Benjy was real popular. The kids were asking about his life. *Amazing* stories! *Great* stuff!

"He told us that his grandfather was the only one-legged man to survive the Titanic. Isn't that something? We all went out clubbing the first night. Benjy opted to stay home. When we came back to the house, Benjy was j'ing off to a birthing documentary he was watching on the Discovery channel. The kids flipped. Then he stole every goddamn item in the house while we were fighting.

"They voted me out. *Of my own damn rented house!* Shit. You were there! You saw it! Total curve ball. Surprised me that the kids would do that! As if it's a reality show! I locked 'em all out and took a Spirit home. Kept the money. But then faced another sitchy when I got home. Had to boot out the Airbnb assholes in my house. Claimed they were here for a funeral. Still don't believe them. They're refusing to pay me. But I *will* get my money. Blood on my knife or shit on my dick, I will collect what I'm owed. So, what was I telling you earlier? It was important. I forget."

When he's reminded, he nods and launches right back into it. "Oh yeah! I've seen every movie M. Night Shyamalan ever made. He's *so* underrated. From what I've read, he's a modest guy. I thought *The Village* was a work of art. I was blown away by that last scene. No planes are allowed to fly over the village. Wow! Consider my mind blown to the bone!"

Randy regally pulls out a well worn piece of yellow, lined paper.

"This is my Underrated List," he says. "I've been keeping it for the longest time. Things that I find underrated and unfairly abused. *Inspector Gadget.* Cheese in the crust pizza. The word 'crispy' to describe something really, really fucking cool. Hermit crabs. *Young* ones. Clean and odorless women. Deaf girls. Not sure why. Maybe they're vulnerable. Wounded birds. Feathers all damaged. Wings all crooked. Feet all *askew*. I *like* dat!

"Billy Baldwin. He's not as puffy as the rest of those jokers. The pasta at American Girl Doll in Tysons. I love the atmosphere. Best-ever chicken tenders, too. I used to go all the time until I was kicked out. Great place to write. The Jamaican beef patties at Suburban Hospital. I'll often pretend a friend has cancer just to eat there. The only part of island culture I like.

"*Who Framed Roger Rabbit. Spider-Man* by U2. Unbelievably underrated. The Phil Collins movie *Buster*. He started out as an actor. No one knows that. He can make really strange faces. He's hilarious. Having sex with a strobe light blasting. Looks like you're moving in slow motion. The Aussie Four Course Meal at the Gaithersburg Outback. The Bloomin' Onions are a famous Australian dish. Cinnamon Schnapps with exactly one ice cube. Has to be a *round* cube with a *center* hole. The Thanksgiving buffet at Mustang's Gentlemens Club. Condoms with polka dots. You can get those at the dollar store. Kid Creole and the Coconuts. Best party music, bar none! The last Huey Lewis album. *Plan B.* Genius. I love indoor hammocks. The mud wrestlers at the Annapolis Renaissance Festival. They're nuts! They throw mud at each other! Makes me laugh like a hyena!"

Randy imitates how a hyena might laugh. It's extremely funny.

After a good thirty seconds, Randy folds his piece of lined, yellow paper and places it back into the deep-set pocket of his shorts. He's been working on the list for years and shall continue to work on it.

He immediately pulls out another piece of lined, yellow paper. It, too, is well worn. "And here are some things I *despise*. You've heard a few already. The Salvation Army. It's a pyramid scam. Overripe oranges. They make me sick. Do gooders. I *hate* do gooders. Keep the good to yourself. It should be clear that *your* good ain't *my* good. Dancing. Hate it. I'm sporting way too huge a pair of sizzlers to dance. Beatles are overrated. Too pleased with themselves. John Lennon was killed by the Cuban government. I don't like homeless without patter or skills. Can you give me something in return? If I'm going to touch your dirty claws when I hand you a dime or a quarter, can you at least make it worth my while? That's why I liked Benjy. Great stories. Until he stole everything. Skin tags. Gross. Brash and arrogant women; dizzy, daffy dames! *Did someone drop you on your vagina when you were a child? Why so angry?* Knowing them is like riding down Splash Mountain but without the water and more of the craziness. Balloon-animal artists. Just give me a goddamn balloon already! Riddles. Just give me the fucking answer already! I'm probably smarter than you are anyway.

"The Slurpee vape flavor. Tastes absolutely nothing like a real 7-Eleven Slurpee. Could be a *lot* more authentic! That creepy Canadian accent. Oh! You know what I really fucking *hate*? Lizards. They! *Suck*!"

Randy is twirling a black fidget spinner between his right thumb and forefinger. He finds this relaxing. He's been doing so for the past hour, even on the drive over, one hand on the wheel. He's also been known to do so while making love. Keeps him "laser focused."

"Let me explain lizards. Where do I even start? I'm an easy gagger. I'm talking odors. Bad smells. I hate walking into public bathrooms. I only do so now for the paper towels. I hate zoos. I hate the smell of animal fecal matter. *Hate* it. Especially if it's not my own. But I *love* animals. And I always wanted a pet. *Dilemma.* I had one before, but he only lasted a day. A capybara, the largest rodent in the world. I fed it a few too many red hot cinnamon candies and it died young.

"What to do? I see a *Fox* report on *lizards.* Very quiet. No harsh smells. Easy to take care of. They live a long time—sometimes *too* long. A lot of bang for the buck. So I go on to Craigslist. A kid in Frederick is selling one. I talk him down from $200 to $100. He throws in a terrarium and all that other crap. I take the lizard home and name him Turk, which is the name of an elementary school friend who later became the ball boy for the Bullets. I don't call them the Wizards. I refuse. To me, they have always been and will always be … the Bullets. End of da mutherfucking story. Turk and I are still great Facebook friends. Yeah, Turk the Lizard is quiet. *Real* fucking quiet. Doesn't do a thing. Tedious.

"But then I'm thinking: *What could such a useless animal be good for?* You ever see all those animals who make millions? The cat who plays the piano? The parrot who takes a shit? All that? I thought: *I want to turn Turk into that.* Make him do something for all of those unwashed pebbles that I'm stealing from the Falls Road public golf course and then putting into his terrarium.

"The great thing about lizards is that they're slow. They allow you to do whatever the fuck you want. Not like dogs. Or cats. Or capybaras. I first tried 'Sad Lizard.' That didn't work. Maybe a few hundred hits. Then I tried 'Happy Lizard.' That didn't work. Turk only looked bored. Then I really studied him. *Who in the hell does he look like?* And you know who he really looked like? I'll tell you."

A young, female jogger approaches. She's attractive.

Randy, as he typically does when confronted with female beauty, offers up his right arm to high-five. It's a bighearted gesture. She passes.

"Girl, I *smell* you," he whispers.

"Excuse me?" she asks, stopping.

"Wanna go halfsies on a baby?" asks Randy, charmingly.

"Are you for real? *What* did you just say?!"

"Nothing. Just sayin' hi is all. Have a *wonderful* day!"

The woman breaks into a jog again, albeit a bit more quickly.

Randy says: "I was being sarcastic. They'll slap half the time. This Betty chose not to. Maybe she didn't see. Maybe she's stuck up. Either way, it's cool. So I'm looking at Turk and I'm stoned from Bennies, really whoosh-zipping, and I see in my mind one of my all-time favorite historical characters: Dirk Diggler. I love that guy. We're so alike. You know why? Because I also *know* what's it like to be different. I don't have a huge cock but I *do* have an oversized personality and a jumbo-sized mind."

Another female jogger approaches. This one, too, is young and attractive. Randy notices but very suavely refuses to make a move.

"Not my type. Too fat. But acceptable face. B, B minus. Which is pretty damn good. Good from far, far from good. She's D.A.D., you know? *Dime a dozen,* baby. So I have a lizard who looks like Dirk Diggler. *Now* what? He doesn't have a huge cock. Not many lizards do. But that's an easy fix.

"I buy the web rights to TurkWiggler.com. No one's already snagged it. Incredible! Just insane. It's the *perfect* name for a lizard porn star! I get some string. Some clay. An adorable tiny red glass bead. I fashion the homemade cock and then strap it on. And it looks *amazing*. Phenomenal. First time in history that a lizard has a colossal choad. Ready to fuck the shit out of anything that crosses its tiny little path. *I just did something even God was never been able to do!*

"I take a million and a half photos. I upload them all to the site. Try to drum up some interest on Twitter and Instagram. Offered T-shirts with Turk Wiggler on it. Cost a fortune! Beer cozies. *Nothing.* Disappointing as hell!

"Then the Animal Cruel Association gets involved, or whatever they're fucking called. Another bunch of do-gooders! They were upset about the fake cock. It was erect. Limp would have fine. Erect wasn't. Too many rules! *Whatever.* I still have the Turk Wiggler T-shirts and bumper stickers, beer cozies, key-chains. You can have 'em all if you're interested. Half off."

He sighs. Over the years, Randy has suffered very few creative failures, but this one, in particular, stings.

"I haven't failed at much. There *was* that time at rock and roll fantasy camp on a Bahamian cruise and I was supposed to shred with Mick Jones from Foreigner but he cancelled at the last minute because his daughter died or something. That was awful. Always dreamed of playing with him on 'Hot Blooded.'

"But look, I think the most important thing is that you just try to keep moving *forward*. I'm tired. Let's head back."

Randy gracefully does a U-turn and starts the long walk back to where he's parked, a quarter mile away in a dirt parking lot. There's a rare sadness in his eyes. But it disappears when an attractive jogger approaches—the same from earlier who refused Randy's kind offer of a high-five.

She, too, is heading back from whence she started.

Randy offers up his muscular hand once again, more forcefully than the first go-round. On his part, there is no hesitation.

On the young woman's face, there is a flicker of hesitation: *Should I or shouldn't I?*

Oh, what the hell!

A decision has been made.

One she will never regret.

The slap is strong.

The noise *resounds*.

"Life works out if you last long enough," Randy declares, a smile back on his handsome face. "The trick is you can't stop. Never, *ever* stop. Hang on a sec. I need to stop. There's a rock in my shoe."

Randy skillfully takes care of the situation and continues talking and walking with his unlaced yellow sneakers.

"I ended up dropping Turk off at the front of the Salvation Army store on the Pike. Left a note in an empty adult diaper box. Idiots called me. Ordered me to pick him back up. That's why I hate the Salvation Army. It's a con. A pyramid scam. Ended up just leaving him in Cabin John Park. But I forgot to take off his fake cock. I think it was still erect! Maybe it'll help him get laid. Ha! *Ha*!"

Randy imitates how a lizard might laugh. It's not difficult to imagine Randy one day opening for his all-time favorite stand-up, Jeff Dunham.

That familiar bounce has returned to Randy's step. Back to the Hummer he walks—nay, *glides*. Dusk is beginning to settle and the buzz of spring cicadas kicks up a notch.

And yet, far away—farther than any average human could ever hope to bridge—Randy has already retreated back into his head, swimming, floating, whirling among his exceptional, careening thoughts.

Ha ha! laughs Randy. *Ha ha!*

One can only look on in enraptured wonder!

[Note: Hey! It's me! Randy! Not Noah. I love women. Man, do I love women! And they love me. But not all ladies are perfect. For instance, here are few things that it would take for me *not* to go out with them. No argument. You break it, you bought it. All sales final!!!!!]

WHAT IT WOULD TAKE TO
NOT GO OUT WITH A GIRL

They listen to NPR

They're too good for "Two and a Half Men"

They have a difficult brother who's going to cause problems

Their starfish is too delicate

They love trees and flowers too much

They don't find Alf funny

They act all haughty when your snake needs milked

They're better at trampolining

They're pregnant with some other dude's whelp

They are "sapiosexual." I don't even know what this means but saw
it on OkCupid and it sounds awful.

Chapter Thirteen:
LOOKIN' GOOD!

"Like *this*, Roger," says Randy, rolling the flyer and placing it through the door handle. "You gotta *place* it where they can *see* it after they arrive home from work. This is *vital*!"

Randy and the Dodger are out canvassing for votes, placing handwritten flyers in locations where neighborhood association voters will be sure to notice them.

Randy expects each of his neighbors to closely study the information throughout the evening, very prudently and with a yellow highlighter, so as to not miss a single significant item.

"The flyer is brilliant," says Randy, not bragging, just stating the obvious. "*101 Reasons Why I'm Better Than Nora As President and Should be President Once Again*. Here," he pulls out a flyer from his back pocket. "*Number one: More fun. Number two: Will lower monthly dues. Number three: Yearly trip to a Nats game, all of us! Dutch treat!*

"Skipping down to number twenty-eight: *Door is always open at my house*. And that's true! Stop by any time to rap, I don't care when! Except when I'm scrumping with my escort! Ha ha!

"Next meeting's soon. I wanted it to take place back at my awesome home but the bitch said no. Nora said it *has* to be her place or no dice. Power crazy. She's collapsing from all the pressure. I can see it in her eyes. Dodger, play that thing."

"What thing, Randy?"

"That thing."

"What thing, Randy?"

Randy leans in to whisper to the Dodger, who smiles broadly.

"I *love* that thing, Randy!"

"Then play it already," says Randy, running out of patience, as there's an entire neighborhood to canvas before Randy's former and beloved constituents arrive home from work. Randy would prefer *not* to talk to them in person.

Not that he doesn't *want* to.

He'd just much rather use his extensive and detailed flyer to do all the work for him.

Roger pulls out a small digital recorder and hits play. It's the entire episode of a *Who's the Boss*.

"No," says Randy, not surprised. "The *other* thing. C'mon, it's getting late."

"Okay, Randy!" says the Dodger, pressing another button. "Okay dokie!"

"*Okie* dokie!" corrects Randy. "It's *okie*! How many goddamn times?!"

"Okay, Randy! Okay *do*-kay!"

"Jesus," says Randy.

"*Jesus*!" says the Dodger.

"I'm going to ask you just one more time—" begins Randy.

This is just the inspiration that the Dodger needs.

Tongue out, the Dodger at last hits the correct memory file.

Randy exclaims: "Finally!"

"*Finally*!" yells the Dodger.

"Yes, finally," says Randy.

"*Finally*!" yells the Dodger.

"Shut!" explains Randy.

From out of the recorder comes the agreeable voice of Randy himself: *"Hi there! I hope I am not disturbing your dinner. This is Randy S._____, calling to discuss a most crucial choice you're going to have to make soon. You know what's meant a lot to me? All those times we attended each other's backyard barbecues, neighborhood association meetings, and watching each other's kids play soccer in the playground.*

What memories! While I don't have a child, I will forever cherish our friendships.

"*Through the years I have enjoyed the friendship of just so many honest, hard-working people. People such as the Taiwanese Leigh C.____ and his lovely but bashful white wife Bets. People like the young Mary Mary and her wonderful Caribbean nurse and caregiver, I'm forgetting her name. People like Arnold Bam Bam and his gorgeous wife, Susan, who, in 2013, helped me organize a neighborhood bake sale, only to see it then blossom into an annual and much-cherished tradition in our development. I believe these bonds were forged and strengthened thanks to one simple thing: Loyalty. Stay loyal. At the next meeting, do the right thing. Choose Randy S._____ as your next association president! Paid for by Randy S._____.*"

The Dodger turns off the recorder.

"Kind of a lie," states Randy. "Mary Mary ain't young. I just call her that. And the bake sale isn't really and truly much cherished. They refused to allow me to bake edibles for it. But the rest was really good, right? I've left that message on most of their cells already. If they pick up and ask 'Who is this?', I pretend I can't hear them. If they hang up, I call right back and just start where I stopped. It's very effective. C'mon, Dodger. We got more houses to hit."

The Dodger rolls a fresh flyer and goes to place it through a door handle, when the door swings open, wildly.

"I don't want one."

"Well," says Randy, smiling diplomatically. "*Every* vote counts, right, Nora?"

"I suppose so, Randy," says Nora.

She doesn't look as if she means it.

"Did you not like my call?" asks Randy.

"You mean your robo call at 2:00 A.M.?" Nora asks, looking a lot older than her forty-three years.

"Wasn't robo," says Randy proudly. "Was personalized. So why aren't you at work? Did you lose your job? Has the presidency sapped too much of your energy? *Harder* than it looks, no?"

"No," says Nora, petulantly. "It's not difficult in the least. My family is arriving from Tampa. I'm prepping for their arrival!"

"Been there once. Slept with a few women from Florida, but not in Tampa. Sad."

"Randy, can you please not call me at 2:00? All I want to do is lead this association the best I'm able. And while you had your … strengths, I feel I have my own strengths as president."

"Let me ask you something, Nora. Do I come to your job and tell you what to do?"

"You don't," says Nora.

"Where do you work?"

"Sibley Hospital."

"Do I come to Sibley Hospital to tell you what to do? Um, what do you do?"

"I'm a pediatric cardiologist specializing in Aortic Valve Stenosis."

Randy has no time for this. "Do I?"

"Do you what?"

"Come to your job and tell you what to do?"

"You do not."

Randy is most pleased with the Socratic method he's adopted for extracting the truth.

It is not difficult to picture Randy lecturing on a grove just outside ancient Athens. "Thank you. So please leave *this* job for *me*. This is a job I was *born* to perform. I was *made* for this."

"You were born to be president because your grandmother—"

"My *Mam-Mam*," interjects Randy.

"Because your Mam-Mam willed this land to you—"

"She was a *special* woman. And I'm a special man. And I sold my Mam-Mam's land to create dreams. I did that out of the kindness of my own heart and not for the money. Well, for the money, too, but mostly out of the kindness of my heart. Made happier by all the money."

Nora appears flummoxed. "I have no doubt she was a special woman," she starts. "But *you* made the laws. It takes a majority of the association to elect a new president. Isn't that right? So the association voted for me. It's a done deal, okay? And I just want to lead the association. Really not too much to ask, right? So now I have to prepare for my family's visit—"

"My mother ran off with a deaf plumber named Chuck," says Randy, sadly.

"I'm … I'm so sorry to hear that."

"Taught me how to deaf sign to Jon Bon Jovi songs."

"That's … fascinating. But I do have to prepare for my family."

"What's up?"

"A wedding to attend this weekend."

"Families are weird, aren't they?" Randy asks.

Nora leans in closer and scrunches her eyes. She's concentrating on what Randy is about to say. This is going to be *good*.

"They're like a big ol' herpes sore. They suck, but everyone has one."

"I …" begins Nora.

Is she too slow to understand what Randy is getting at?

"My PopPop was a difficult man," goes on Randy. "He stood in the tunnel and nearly watched me die. Not a nice thing for him to do."

Nora squints harder.

"PopPop's side wanted to turn this farm into a park. A *playground*. They claimed that there was this *special* spider. It was protected. That, *even if I wanted to,* I couldn't sell this farm! Because that *special* spider lived right here on the land. I took care of *that* special problem, *believe* me!"

Randy motions as if shooting down a row of spiders with a machine gun.

"Wah *wah*! Bang *bang*! Bye *bye*!"

Randy put down the imaginary machine gun. He launches back into his amazing tale:

"But I held firm. And I sold the land in order for the good people of this area like you and Arthur and Leigh to live on this land. And I think that was an honorable choice. I'm very proud of myself."

Randy pats his own back.

"*Proud*!" says the Dodger.

"Assholes," says Nora.

"Definitely," says Randy. "Families *are* assholes."

"No. Everyone has an *asshole*. Not a herpes sore," says Nora. "Not necessarily."

"Wouldn't be so quick to generalize, Nora. But yeah, assholes. I guess everybody *does* have an asshole. I never thought of that. The human body! Tis a wonder, ain't it?"

"It sure is," says Nora, attempting to close the door. "*Tis a wonder.*"

Randy sticks his huge, powerful foot inside the door jam.

"Nora?" he asks, not the least bit plaintively.

"Yes?"

"One last request, okay? That the next meeting takes place at my town home, okay? That's all I'm asking. I miss everyone. *Please.* Just let me have this, okay? Let me have the next meeting. That's all I'm asking."

Nora sighs as if this is a burden too huge for her to accept and not just a simple, modest request from a beloved former president who wants nothing more than to re-connect, if only for the night, with his beloved ex-constituents, many of whom miss the fun and the joy and the unbridled excitement Randy always brought to the job, not that it was a job, per se, but more of a moral—almost religious—calling.

"Fine," says Nora. "Next meeting at your place. If not the next meeting, then the next party. But you'll allow me to govern, right? In peace? No more interference? No more 2:00 A.M. fake robo calls? No more canvassing with flyers?"

"I shall," says Randy, nobly.

Randy goes to pull his foot out of the door jam but stops at the last second.

"Yes, Randy?"

"Thank you, Nora," Randy exclaims, bowing most majestically, one pinkie extended in an impish royal manner.

Perhaps Nora is taken aback by this incredible display of elaborate 18th century courtesy. Where could Randy have ever learned such a move?

It's a fascinating question but Nora does not seem to be interested in its origin. Perhaps she's just not the curious type.

The answer, for now, will remain unspoken but no less impressive: the 2011 cinematic classic, *Your Highness,* starring Zooey Deschanel and James Franco.

Whatever the case—and after Randy graciously removes his tremendous foot—Nora closes the door quickly.

"*Tis a wonder*!" screams the Dodger. "*The human body*!"

"Let's go, moron," says Randy. "You have some calls to make."

"*Me*, Randy?"

"Throat hurts," says Randy. "And I have to watch the Caps at Hoops. Want to get there before the dickhead government workers arrive. All those fucking dickhead government workers who don't work for a living."

Randy and the Dodger walk towards Randy's $1.5 million town home. They disappear over the horizon, backlit by a gorgeous sunset, two heroes pounding the pavement so selflessly for the betterment of all of humanity.

The Dodger goes to high-five Randy.

Randy continues on, as he must, a man alone, too burdened by his own pressing demands.

Or is he?

This time the high-five *is* answered.

It's a beautiful sight to behold!

Beyond that, as if he doesn't have enough on his plate, Randy has been struggling to finish his epic song about his experiences at this year's Spring Break. He hopes to create a timeless classic that will capture, for all eternity, what exactly went on this past year.

It would be based, in concept, on one of Randy's favorites, "Wreck of the Edmund Fitzgerald" by Gordon Lightfoot. Randy finds this song fun.

But his particular epic is not coming along so effortlessly or enjoyably.

Being an artist is difficult. Randy could easily skate through life enjoying the pleasures that he can so easily afford—thanks to Mam-Mam.

That he has not—that he has chosen to take the more difficult route—says more about Randy than any memoir possibly could, no matter the page count.

As for this new epic song, there are *so* many choices.

How to begin?

How to end?

What exactly to rhyme with "turd"?

Should Randy mention the evening spent at Bomba Ray's eating chicken nuggets?

Should Randy mention winning the karaoke contest with an amazing rendition of Styx's "Renegade"?

Or would that be *bragging*?

The choices are endless … but as this great man walks into the distance, he is confident that he will be able to pull it off.

And why shouldn't he?

A marvel, this man they call "Randy."

A man for today.

A man for tomorrow.

A man for … forever.
Go, go Randy!!!!!!!!!!!!!!!

[Note: This is Randy, not Noah. I have to admit that I struggled with the following song. It was not easy to write. And yet I couldn't be happier with the result. It's called "Ain't No Way to Make a Lasting Memory at Will Last Forever and Ever." The title is beautiful, as is the song itself. I finished the lyrics at around 5:30 A.M. as the sun was rising. I was smoking a bowl of cheap-ass hash my friend Tonker stole for me. I could see birds off in the distance. I think they were birds. I wonder if they'd ever want to hear it? I'm not an egomaniac but it's really good. It's on the next page. If you want to sing it professionally, just contact me and I'm sure that we can work out a deal!]

Got a groovy tale to tell and it's gonna be told now!
I guarantee you that it's gonna make you go "wow!"
You ain't gonna believe a g-damn word!
Unless you ain't nothin' less than a g-damn turd!

So …

Benji … just a dude who lived on da damn street,
Outside that store that made me dat buttery bis-keeeet!
Started off real cool but kind of lost his sheeeeeeeet!
Up to five bottles a day, had a legless relative on the Titan-eeeeec.
Jacked off while watching a woman giving birth,
Said he'd never done so before but I don't think it was his first.
But enough about him, let's talk about someone better.
I'm talking about me, that'd be R-A-N-D-Y—
that's me to the fucking letter!

Did my very best to hide my yellow choppers,
Tried my very best to hide my sagging whoppers,
Did my very best to hide all of my lower grays.
Didn't tell a single lady that I'm what the docs might call "spayed."

Played Frisbee, played quarters,
played drinking games, hoovered up dunes of snorters!
Purchased a rack of rubbers, bought buckets of lube,
Saw more than my share of young, fresh boob!

But not all was wonderful—I only slept with two Bettys,
Not like in the past when I was motherfuckin' legendary.
Yeah, this Spring break didn't go as planned
Here's the thing:

One had a stanky ass, I hate to be crass,
Cause her cooch smelled like a pooch and her ass smelled like a gash!

**--Written by Randy S._____, copyright by Randy S._____,
transcribed by Noah B.**

Chapter Fourteen: FIRST KISS!

Randy has *always* had amazing ideas that are above and beyond what other people might consider "normal." Compared with others, Randy has just always thought *differently*.

"I'm not saying I think *better*. Just *different*. I'm an outside-the-box thinker. This is not me bragging. This is just the god's honest truth."

Randy sits in his big fluffy recliner down in his finished basement, next to the framed and signed jersey of Art Monk, his all-time favorite Redskin.

He's on the phone: "I bet you are filthy. Filthy little firecracker. No, no … hey! *Why so upset?* Sure, I can hold." He rolls his eyes as if he's been through this before and will, no doubt, be through this again: "Goddamn I.R.S. Just wanna know if my Jet Ski is tax deductible if I drove it into a pier. I'll call back after I television."

He hangs up.

Randy's recliner has five pockets for remotes, as well as a cup holder and a vibrating foot massage. It is clearly top of the line. "This hole over here is big enough to hold a Big Gulp," Randy brags. "That's a big-ass hole!"

With his universal remote, Randy mutes his 78-inch plasma TV and the audio for *Two and a Half Men* goes silent.

Randy sighs.

"When I started this memoir, I promised I'd always be totally honest. What I'm about to tell you, I haven't told anyone else. You ready?"

Randy stares at the ceiling. And then goes deep:

"When I was a kid, I invented a magical land called Zyngïa."

He pauses to see if there might be a reaction from his listener. When he finds that there is not, he continues:

"Zyngïa is an enchanted kingdom a lot like Narnia but looking more like suburban Maryland. There is only one way to enter into this magical world: through a secret portal that only I know about. When I was twelve, the portal was located in the shitter in the school's bathroom. Just pretend anyway.

"I wrote a book about all this. I'm the king. *King Randy.* Everything in Zyngïa takes place exactly one day previous to our own reality. It all gets so confusing! There are a lot of creatures. The two most powerful are the Wides and the Shorts. Wides have been fighting the Shorts for eons over a slice of magical forest called Renfruck. Renfruck is weird. It snows upwards and people talk backwards, and the guards—the Renfruckers—are incredibly strong but they don't have much patience. They're hot heads. Like Italians or Greeks but without the full heads of hair.

"So I'm the king of Zyngïa and I'm trying to capture Renfruck from the Wides. I'm the best king the land has ever seen. Bring the recorder closer to my face please. There's a boy.

"I open fast food restaurants and I open motels. I open everything. I believe in commercialism. I even invite Aerosmith to play down there. The real Aerosmith, not the cover band Dream On. Just pretend. They say yes, but for a million Zyngïan dollars. I can afford it! I oust the previous king, a real loser, a talking lion who slept all day and played with himself in his castle. I make the asshole move into a small condo I built on the outskirts of Zyngïa. His name is Bennett. The Zyngïan water park is named after me. Bennett works concessions. I figured I'd give the fat fuck something to do. The teens down in Zyngïa throw curly fries at Bennett. The curly fries get stuck in his dirty, twiggy mane!

"Okay. So back to this world. It's summer in Maryland. I'm like fourteen. As usual, I'm impressing all of the neighborhood kids who used Mam-Mam's farm as an informal playground.

"I'm a magnet for kids who love to see me doing all sorts of crazy shit, like jumping off a house and into a mound of hay, or riding my Huffy over ramps I built from wood stolen from the new houses going up all around the farm, or flinging Mam-Mam's diabetic socks at hornets' nests and running like hell.

"One day, I'm kicking at an annoying fire ant colony. I'm not wearing shoes. The kids are impressed and laughing like crazy. I'm having so much fun I forget all about the stings. It's a few weeks later and my foot is now infected. It stinks like an old ketchup bottle left out in the sun. Or a bellybutton you forget to clean for the entirety of tenth grade, which later happens to me. It just doesn't smell good. Like old crabs in a scented trash bag.

"Mam-Mam takes me to the clinic at the back of the CVS and the hot ethnic nurse tells me I have to rest. So that's when I pretty much spend the rest of the summer in bed looking out the window, watching kids play on Mam-Mam's farm like you would in a movie or a TV show.

"I notice a girl. She's my age. *Is she new?* I like her look. A tomboy. I learn that her name's Melanie; she goes by Mel. She's just starting to develop her buds. Meaning she was just beginning to develop. Everyone knew it. *I have got to meet this girl!*

"Mam-Mam lets me out of the house at the end of August. I limp confidently over to where this girl Mel's sitting on a mound of dirt. Even then, I'm great with girls. 'What's with the foot?' she asks. She's chewing gum. It smells like wild apples.

"I already have an answer locked and loaded: 'I got stabbed at a fight in the Sub Standard.' The Sub Standard was a take-out restaurant inside the food court at Montgomery Mall. The restaurant's real name was the Sub Supreme, but no one called it that. They had substandard tuna from some Chinese country but they put a ton of tuna on each sub, so I ate there all the time.

"I forget what Mel says. It was something like, 'Wow! I am so fucking *incredibly* impressed! You must be so fucking brave and strong! You are so incredible! Do you want to come swimming with me?' It was something like that. Luckily, Mel doesn't ask how the fight ends, which is good. I don't have an answer locked and loaded for that one.

"Mel leads me into the rich development next to the farm, where she lives. The house is huge and has its own pool. Her father was a government lobbyist. I strip down to my tighties and I do my best to hide the scar and the lingering odor coming from my left foot. I jump into the pool and wait for Mel to come out. She's changing into a Minnie Mouse one piece. Soon we're splashing and having an awesome time. The Soup Dragons are blasting on a boom box. I hate that band. I hate any band who wears bucket hats and who are white.

"We come together in the shallow end and kiss. It lasts for a few seconds. Mel smells like farm. Not dirty goat hay but more like the clean, rural straw you'd find on the porch of a Cracker Barrel where I like to relax. She's wearing pink lip gloss. Tastes like honey. I pop a bone. A tiny bone but definitely a bone. A baby bone. It's all very innocent.

"This ain't my first kiss even though I'm only fourteen. Not by a long shot. I may have been a pony jockey but this twasn't my first ride! But it's *hers*. She loves it and wants to kiss all night! I do a great job. I leave the pool for dinner. The sun's beginning to set and I'm still popping a tiny one. It points homeward. Always follow your bone. I can see Mel's mother standing on the lawn as I leave. I wave happily. She doesn't wave back. Maybe she's seen my bone?

"School's starting soon. I knock on Mel's window every night and leave her love notes. I write them on Mam-Mam's prescription papers I find lying around the farm house. Mel thinks I'm writing 'vagina' but they really read 'angina.'

"I learn to play Ozzy songs on the slide-whistle. I sit in the tree next to Mel's bedroom and play all night, until her mom comes out to yell at me to go home. *Bitch.*

"School starts. I see Mel in the hallways and yet she never says anything. *Nothing.* Not even a nod. Not even the slightest hint of facial recognition. Her friends would look at me and laugh, but not her.

"I wasn't what one might call *popular.* I think I was too smart for the rest of the idiots. My intelligence wasn't traditional. It wasn't *grade* intelligence so much as *creative* intelligence. I was a creative genius. That scared people."

Randy stops. He's done for the day. He'll pick up with this *amazing* story at a later date.

"I'm going to unmute this now. I'm lonely," he says, hitting the remote MUTE button.

For now, there's a fresh repeat of *Two and a Half Men* to watch.

Didja know!
Randy is double-jointed but only on his right foot?!

An Outsider's Perspective!

John Papageorgiou, owner of Poolesville Vape: "A biography? Of Randy? That's ... what do you want to know? He comes in about twice a month. Has his favorites. Sometimes he'll just hang. Did he tell you about the time he was arrested for receiving a blowjob inside a breast-feeding pod at Dulles airport? This was a few years back. He was flying to Florida for Spring Break. He'd just met the teen at the airport's Auntie Anne's. Cops dragged his ass out of there. I don't know what else to say. Randy."

Chapter Fifteen:
ABRA CADABRA!

Randy is sitting at an indoor table within Potbelly Sandwich Works, overlooking the gorgeous man-made lake at Rio Mall in Gaithersburg, Maryland. It's one of Randy's favorite spots to reminisce. The fake lake and fake trees and fake ducks floating on the fake lake put him at ease.

It's lunchtime and Randy is talking about his childhood crush, Melanie, or Mel, his first "real" girlfriend, from seventh grade. He's nibbling on his Grilled Chicken and Cheddar, with extra cheddar. Randy has an insatiable appetite for top-notch food, as well as for knowledge. To Randy, this is the very best sandwich in the entire Washington area.

His voracious grunts attest to this fact.

"I forget where we left off. You interrupted me. Okay, so we had an unfortunate falling out," Randy says, voice slightly tinged with regret. "Mel and I broke up. Or she broke up with me. I can't remember. But I do remember thinking, *What is the one thing I can do now to impress Mel?* You know? *Like what could I possibly do to get her interested in me again?*"

Randy brightens.

"Can you guess? It's an easy answer. It really is. That one very special thing that would win Mel back into my good graces? Every guy does it ..."

Randy waits for the answer he is sure to arrive, but doesn't. Then Randy helpfully provides the answer to his very own complicated riddle:

"*Magic*. Right? *All* girls love magic, of *any age*. When a guy pulls off a magic trick it's ... it's the equivalent of being great in bed. Quick hands. A surprising outcome. Women gasp. And then *applaud*. If you're *really* good!

"Fall Talent Show was coming up in October and I'm endlessly practicing. I'm The Great Randoni. The day arrives. I'm on third. Up first was a white girl twirling a flag. And then a black kid doing somersaults. I could have watched all this for free on television. My turn arrives. 'I'm Your Boogie Man' begins to blast, my all-time fave. The crowd goes fucking *insane*.

"I stroll out wearing a top hat and a fancy cape Mam-Mam fashioned from out of old bed sheets. It's red and white. There's a Strawberry Shortcake on the back. I'm holding a wand, something Mam-Mam slapped together, a ruler painted black. The top hat is real. Mam-Mam bought it at a magic store in Kensington. I have it to this day. Although it's gotten super funky with mildew.

"The place explodes. Everyone's laughing. Admit it: Not many kids would have the twizzlers to get up on stage to perform magic. I remember thinking, *Damn it to hell! I wish Mam-Mam was here and not at the VFW playing speed bingo!*

"I announce, 'Mel! Where are you?! You are the *luckiest* person in this auditorium because you are going to be my assistant!'

"All of Mel's friends laugh and point at her. She blushes and mimes, *No! No! Please no!* But it's so clear she's only pretending to be embarrassed. Like, *Oh man, please don't pick me!* but also really wanting to be picked, you know? She slowly makes her way to the stage.

"I launch into the fabulous patter that all great magicians are known for: 'What would y'all think if I told you I had a rabbit in this hat?' There is a collective cry from the crowd. They've never seen anything like this. They are going *bezerk*.

"I remove my top hat and make a great production of showing it to the audience. Top, then bottom. They see nothing but an empty hat. Just like the Great Randoni wants them to. I've got them in the palm of my magic hand. I can feel a buzz. *Electric*.

"I glance over to Miss T._____, the English teacher who hates my guts for once saying her breath stank like dog shit. Even *she* is smiling. Mel climbs up on to the stage, acting all coy. Pretending she'd rather be *anywhere* else. *Right.* I hand her the hat and whisper, 'Okay, on the count of three, this is what I want you to do: I want you to pull the rabbit from out of the hat. It's behind a hidden compartment!'

"Mel's eye is twitching all fast and flittery from the excitement. *Twitch! Twitch! Twitch!* It's obvious nothing like this has ever happened to her before.

"I begin the countdown. 'One!'

"The audience screams '*One!*'

"I say 'Two!'

"The audience screams, '*Two!*'

"I pause.

"The anxiety is unbearable.

"As cool as can be, as cool as the coolest of Las Vegas professional magicians, I yell 'THREE!!!!'

"I shake the hat one last time for show. I nod to Mel. She starts pulling the rabbit out of the hat …"

Randy shudders at the memory. He takes another bite from his Chicken and Cheddar, and a long swig from his extra-large Mountain Dew. This is not an easy story for him to finish …

But it's apparent that he has little choice. To this day, more than two decades after the fact, what *is* clear is that this is a story Randy *must* tell.

Randy bravely decides to goes all in with the story, spelunking into the deepest and darkest crevices of his own memory bank:

"The audience screams. I look over to the rabbit. *Uh oh, he ain't lookin' so hot, you kow?—*

"Hang on. Let me just swallow this. Don't wanna choke. I once nearly choked to death in a Chinese restaurant. Tried to swallow the entire fortune cookie at once. Lost that bet. With the bus boy. He won. What can I say? We all have our Vietnam."

Randy swallows, takes a swig from his drink and then continues:

"See, I had found this rabbit living down by the creek. It was a free creek rabbit. I fed it Bacobits and Reese's Peanut Butter cups so it had enough to eat. He was a big boy. But creek rabbits aren't as healthy as *pet store* rabbits. I *know* that *now*.

"Ask anyone who owns a creek rabbit. They're basically *used*. They break down. They age faster. It's like people who live on the streets. Anyway, this rabbit dies on me up on stage. But they're performers! That's the risk they take!

"Anyway, this one is dead. Mel begins to cry. I can't blame her. Half of the girls would have done the same. I'm not angry. The teacher whose breath smelled like dog shit, Miss T. _____, is weeping. The rabbit is hanging there, dead. Mr. H. _____, the principal, runs up and grabs the rabbit to see if it's real. It is. He drops the rabbit and runs off the stage. He later took some time off to 'rest' in Arizona. The audience is fleeing. Miss T._____ is gagging. Mel jumps off the stage and runs toward the exit. Her friends are comforting her. *Boo hoo, boo hoo!*

"I'm still up on that stage, holding a bleeding, dead rabbit. I don't know why it's bleeding. What the hell am I supposed to do *now*? I'm all alone. Typical. *Thanks for the help, everyone!* I'm being sarcastic.

"Months pass. *So now what?* What do I need to do now to impress Mel? I'm in a really deep pickle here. How do I crack this estrogen puzzle? Magic is out of the picture. It's usually foolproof but not with Mel. She's a tough crack to crack.

"How do I get back in Mel's good graces? Can you guess? It's an easy answer. It really is. That one very special thing that would win back any girl? Let me tell you, okay? Girls *all* want to be *princesses*. It's obvious. So that's easy! No problem at all! I've already created a magical kingdom! How much more work will it take for me to make Mel a princess? I will make Mel a princess in my magical world of Zyngïa! *Simple*! *Presto*!

"I quickly write up a fresh chapter of *The Zyngïan Chronicles*. Chapter fifty something. The next morning, before anyone is awake, I walk to the 24-hour copying place run by the albino and print out three hundred copies. Then I walk the half mile back to Winston Churchill and slip one copy into each locker. I finish as the first students begin to arrive.

"I carefully watch their reactions. They know it's me because I signed each one of the stories 'By Randy S.____.' I receive a lot of looks. Some are like *I can't believe someone so quiet could possibly write something so great*! And others are like *I'm not surprised at all*! And a few are more like: *What a weirdo*! Typical.

"I'm in my Algebra class when I hear a knock. It's a student I don't know, Noelle L._____. She has a cleft lip but was otherwise okay. I'd give her a B, maybe a B-minus, which isn't bad. She motions to me. The teacher, Mrs. Z.____ , says, 'Randy, you are wanted in the principal's office.'

"I'm thinking, *Mel just read the chapter and is so impressed, she went straight to the principal's office*! *And he's also so impressed*! *I'm going to be praised*! *This has never happened before*! *This feels great*!

"But as soon as I walk into the office, I can see that he is *not* happy. Mel is nowhere to be seen. It's just Mr. J._____, the new principal now that Mr. H._____ is out in Arizona getting *psychiatric* help. He used to be the vice principal. This guy hates me, too. Typical. He's screaming loud, practically spitting.

"He's yelling, *'You have gone far beyond the bounds, Randy! You have gone way too far this time! You have embarrassed Mel greatly!'*

"'Wait!' I say, all cool, just as calm as ever. I ask, 'Where's Mel? I want to talk with her.'

"He tells me that Mel threw up in Hallway B and called her

mother to be picked up early. He says that Mel *hated* my story. She's now home resting. I can't talk with her. Not now. *Not ever.*"

Randy pulls out the chapter in question. Even at the age of thirty-four, Randy does not require reading glasses. Like the rest of his body, except for his left knee, torn years ago while participating in an illegal mixed-martial-arts competition on a basketball court on top of a donkey behind the Rockville YMCA, his eyes are in perfect shape.

Randy skims over the chapter quickly. He has long ago memorized most of it anyway. The papers are wrinkled and worn and torn. It is easy to tell just how important this manuscript remains to Randy.

"I shouldn't have written all those romantic scenes involving Mel. That was really the bug in the ointment. One fuck scene took place in a horse stable. Another on top of a drawbridge. Another at a jousting tournament, in the bleachers. I also described Princess Mel's pussy as being like 'the fiery gates of Zomoloff.'

"But," continues Randy, smiling, "what Mr. J. ____, nor anyone else understood, was that this was a major *compliment*. The fiery gates of Zomoloff are *beyond* gorgeous. People go mad looking at them. But how would any of the teachers know all this, never having read the *Chronicles of Zyngïa?* And it's not as if I didn't leave them copies! I slipped a copy into each teacher's mailbox that morning. The idiots were just too *lazy* to read 'em! I never had much luck with teachers. Or cops. Or lifeguards. Or dentists. Or the I.R.S. Or people who work in airports.

"So cut to a few years later. Mel and I are now in 11th grade. Mel's mother is looking out her kitchen window. She'd sometimes notice me peeking into Mel's bedroom, through the curtains. Or trying to glance into the house as they all ate dinner and I'd be strolling past, holding binoculars. Her mom would shoo me away. Nothing more than an annoying bug.

"This time, Mel's mother sees me and I'm lying on the lawn wearing a straw boater and black socks. That's all I'm wearing. I'd just dropped a tab of acid that my friend's older brother, Skitch, gave me. The tab had on it an image of Bart Simpson wearing a sombrero and giving the curse finger. How cool is *that*?!

"The cop who arrested me said, 'You looked like an idiot.' We later used that against him in court. So that worked out well."

Randy smiles in remembrance of this delightful youthful indiscretion. "I came to believe that I was truly living in Zyngïa! It was terrifying! To be fair to Mel's mother, I would have *also* been scared if I saw me lying nude on that lawn, spooking off blotter acid whipped up in a shed by a guy who was brain damaged from a sledding accident!

"I lost touch with Mel," Randy announces sadly, now gathering up his Potbelly Sandwich Works trash and pocketing a few dozen mustard packets for his own fridge. "I moved on. She went off to college and then god knows where. And I did my incredible thing. But I never did forget about her."

Randy is now noisily nibbling on a Potbelly Dream Bar.

He considers this special dessert one of the very finest in the entirety of the Washington, D.C. area.

"Ah, that's life," says Randy, shrugging. "All right, let's head home after I do something important."

Striding confidently up to the cashier, Randy makes a sad face and holds what remains of the Dream Bar in front of him.

"Not cool," he exclaims.

"Excuse me?" asks the young female worker, playing it dumb.

"Manager," says Randy. "I don't deal with flunkies. *Manager.* Now."

"Would you like a new Dream Bar?" asks the worker. "Were you not happy with that one? Did it melt?"

The worker acts as if she's put out and that it isn't her job to make *all* customers happy, especially on a crowded Saturday afternoon with three children's parties taking placing concurrently.

"Can't I help you?" continues the young woman, plaintively.

It's obviously beyond her pay grade.

"*Man. Ah. Jer,*" says Randy slowly. "You know? Like your *boss*? Like the person in *charge*? Of *you*?"

"I'll get him," says the worker.

"Finally," says Randy, uncomplainingly. "God, it takes forever for some people to get what you want, you know? I just assume they can read my mind. They can't. You see, the main thing about women is that—"

"Hello, Randy," says a middle-aged man wearing a name tag that reads ASSISTANT MANAGER. "How can we be of help to you today?"

"Wasn't cold enough," says Randy. "Typically I'd insist that I see the manager but I'm in a rush today. So … I'll deal with you, I guess. I'll deal with a lesser. What I want is a new one please."

"The manager isn't working today. Just me. And I can give you a coupon for a free one next time. You know that."

"Then I'm sorry to say I *must* talk with the owner."

"Of this store?"

"The one, the only."

"That wouldn't be possible, Randy."

"And why wouldn't that be possible?"

"Because it's a corporation. A publicly traded restaurant chain. Out of Chicago."

"I'm sorry?" Randy cocks his ear closer.

"A publicly traded restaurant chain."

"*Publicly traded*, you said?"

"Yes."

"You mean, *with stock*?"

"Yes."

"With *shareholder* meetings?"

The assistant manager suppresses what looks to be a grin. Perhaps he doesn't quite know who he's dealing with.

Like a sucker would with a pool shark.

"Do you know who you're playing with?" Randy finally asks.

"I do," the assistant manager says. "At least I *think* I do."

"I don't *think* you do. Take a *closer* look."

The assistant manager takes a closer look. But he's *still* not quite getting it.

"You're looking at the *owner*," Randy says, perhaps feeling sorry for his prey. There's only so long a barn cat can play with a smaller critter. "Because you're wasting my time, okay? I own one share of stock. And that makes me *part* owner. So, as your *part owner*, I'd love for you to get me a new Dream Bar please. Not a coupon. But a *real* one. *Now*."

The man's smile fades. *Now* he knows who he's dealing with.

"I didn't realize I was talking with the owner," says the man. "Apologies. Sincerely. I'll go get you a fresh Dream Bar *immediately*."

Randy nods, and then makes the traditional hand motion of the pope. He's seen this special move while watching the 1978 classic movie *Foul Play* and has always wanted to use it.

Later, back in his Hummer, one hand on his fresh Dream Bar, the other playing with his fidget spinner, and his right knee steering, Randy lets out a huge laugh.

"The king in his *kingdom*, baby," he says, smiling. "The king in his goddamn motherfucking kingdom!"

RANDY'S ULTIMATE DINNER PARTY GUESTS

Jim Belushi

Chris Barron of the Spin Doctors

Shawn Wayons

The guy who invented cheese in the crust pizza

That's it

Chapter Sixteen:
A WORKING LUNCH!

"*Oooooh*! I just *adore* this skirt!" exclaims Randy. "Isn't it *delightful*?!"

And then softer, Randy murmurs: "I only talk this way so they won't kick me out. I have to pretend to be really excited. If you don't have a kid, you see, you have to really *overdo* it."

It is morning and Randy is flitting about the American Girl Doll store in Tysons Corner, Virginia. He is holding his Felicity doll and "looking" for clothing and accessories. Randy is extremely familiar with the store's layout.

"My cover story," says Randy, searching the sunglass display for a perfect pair, "is that I'm just a huge fan of dolls. Maybe I'm gay. Who cares? It's all undercover." His voice rises: "Ooooh! These are *adorable*!"

Randy chooses a pair of aqua starry glasses for 18-inch dolls, and holds them up to the light, inspecting them with great care. "You have to buy at least one item," he says, by way of explanation. "This will be mine today. When I was here last, a few months ago, I purchased a sequined pom beanie. I told Beth Anne, who usually works the register, that my Felicity's head was cold in the winter."

Standing a few feet away from Randy is a little girl out shopping with her mother. Randy nods over to the both of them, and they both intently stare at Randy's doll, Felicity.

"Here all the time," explains Randy to them, in a very non-threatening voice. "Show's over. I'm not a freak."

The woman looks down and mumbles an apology.

"Besides," says Randy, winking at the girl, "shouldn't you be in school?"

"I'm *thick*!" announces the girl in a lisp, coughing to prove as much.

"Sure you are," says Randy, now winking at the mother. "Get better, kiddo. Okay, let's buy these glasses," he continues, "and visit the restaurant. I'm fucking famished."

Randy walks to the cashier, whose name tag reads *Beth Anne.*

"Hello, Randy," she announces. "Haven't seen you in awhile."

"Busy with a ton of projects," explains Randy. "And waiting for the court case to settle. It's finally done. I can now breathe a huge sigh of relief."

"ACLU?" asks Beth Anne.

"Righto," says Randy. And then: "No need for a bag. Will just slip these in my shirt pocket. Will slap them on Felicity when we eventually get outside. When I put sunglasses on her indoors she tends to get a headache!"

Beth Anne nods. She understands. "What has Felicity been up to?" she asks. She seems genuinely curious.

"She's loving the loft bed and ottoman I got her." Randy laughs. "She keeps telling me that she wishes I bought it for her years and years ago! She's cheeky!"

Beth Anne can only agree. "Did I not I tell you that she would love it? Didn't I say that?"

"For months," answers Randy. "*You did.* I can't deny it!"

"Is Felicity hitting the hair salon today?" ask Beth Anne.

"Not today," explains Randy. "Too much to do! And I love her hair just a little messy. It's cute."

Beth Anne hands Randy back his change. He only pays in cash, a habit he picked up after deciding, at the age of twenty-eight, to no longer pay the absurd, exorbitant late charges on his credit cards, all of which were later confiscated after Randy successfully filed for Chapter Seven.

"Enjoy," says Beth Anne, handing over the tiny pair of sunglasses.

Randy nods, places them in his shirt pocket, grabs Felicity off the counter where she's been resting after her exhausting shopping excursion, and heads on over to the American Girl Doll restaurant.

"Beth Anne just mentioned the ACLU case," says Randy. "I should probably get that into the book. It's also been mentioned in the local papers."

"Table for two?" asks the *maitre d*, standing in front of a large sign that reads: WELCOME TO THE AMERICAN GIRL DOLL CAFÉ!

"*Three*," says Randy, motioning to Felicity.

"Ah," says the *maitre d*, a teen with a bob haircut. She grabs three menus. "Right."

Randy is led over to a table by the window, overlooking the indoor mall. This is his favorite spot. "Thank you," he says, taking a seat and placing Felicity in a child's chair provided by the restaurant. He pulls out his MacBook Air from his *Bearded Clam Ocean City Maryland* tote bag and presses the ON button.

"Potbelly is great but too crowded. So the ACLU," he continues. "As much as I hate them, they kind of saved my ass."

Randy spreads his work papers out on the table. "They allowed me to return here. The Nazis who own this dump weren't exactly thrilled that I was doing some of my best writing in this restaurant. But I *love* it here. I hate Starbucks. Too many fakers jotting down garbage in their *writing journals*."

Randy pronounces "writing journals" in a squeaky, high-pitched voice. It's very humorous.

"But this is where I can *truly* get work done. Place is a ghost town during school hours. Have it *all* to myself. And the best part—"

"Randy!" says a middle-aged waiter, with the name tag *Bruce*. "Long time no *pee* you!"

"Ha!" says Randy. "Bruce! My main man! How *blows* it?!"

"Blows *hard*!" answers Bruce. "Settling in for the day?"

"Working on a book," answers Randy. "A new chapter, anyway."

"Always up to *something*," says Bruce. "Who's your friend? Typically, you're a solo flier!"

"Just my biographer," answers Randy, nonchalantly. "I guess it *has* been awhile. He's writing my memoir. I've been laid real low by your stupid management. But the ACLU took care of *that* problem."

Randy pretends to wash his hands. *Swish, swash. All clean.*

"Yup. They proved that I was as entitled to be here as *anyone* else. As long as I was *truly* interested in shopping here. And that I didn't bother a soul. So I'll just buy one doll item from here on out. Who cares?"

"Not me," says Bruce. "What you having today? The usual?"

"Yes. Best-ever chicken tenders. Mustard in a small bowl. Separate. Not ketchup. I hate ketchup. The smell reminds me of my foot in the ninth grade. Pomodoro pasta, also naked. Butter on the side. I'll get dessert later."

"I'm on it," says Bruce. "And for your friend?"

"He'll have the triple-stacked grilled cheese," Randy says expertly. "And make sure it's *triple* stacked. Last time it was double stacked. Thank you."

"You got it, my brother!" Bruce says, making his way back to the kitchen with the detailed order.

"The advantage of coming to a restaurant where only kids order is that they're used to picky eaters," explains Randy. "And I'm a picky eater. I'm not afraid to admit that. It makes me no less of a man. I hate spices and shit. I like things *plain*. To actually *taste* the food I'm eating. Isn't that its damned purpose? It *is*."

Randy places his MacBook Air on the table. He opens a Microsoft Word document.

"Have a *ton* of work to do," he states. "First item: deal with that stupid writing teacher—if you can even call her that—at the Bethesda Writing Shitter. Going to explain to her again, like one would a child, why I'm a great writer. And why she's *not*. And why I will *never* apologize for showing my movie. She claims she suffered an unwarranted and distressing episode after seeing my porn parody. *Fuck her.* She wants me to give her a trigger warning? *I'll give her a fucking trigger warning!* Right on her *face*!

"And you know what? She lied. She never did send my poems to her agent. She's a *fake.* So I'll publish 'em myself. Big whoop! Okay. Here we go. How does this sound?"

Randy clears his throat and begins to tap out his written response to the teacher:

"'Gee, I'm so sorry that my movie caused you to feel uncomfortable. I'm being sarcastic. Next time, before you criticize, why don't you try to actually *finish* the movie first? I'm a professional writer with hundreds and hundreds of credits, and a very successful Twitter page. I have 35,000 followers. In comparison, the Salvation Army has 15,000 followers. I only paid for 22,000 of those followers. What have you ever published beyond a shitty book of poems on genocide that was positively reviewed in the *Washington Post*? More like the *Washington Compost*! And I'm not even mentioning everything else I've ever accomplished. Did I tell you about the Muffkins? They're like Smurfs but sexier. I invented them. You got Ballerina Muffkin. Writer Muffkin. Mayor Muffkin. I'm very inclusive. Women can do anything. Hot nurse Muffkin. Hot secretary Muffkin. Hot elementary school teacher Muffkin. I'm trying to think. Who else? Housecleaner Muffkin—"

"And we are *back*! With some yummy tummy dishes!" Bruce stands before the table, carrying a ceramic plate of best-ever chicken tenders, cooked to perfection, with the mustard, as requested, on the side. "And … a *triple* stacked grilled cheese for Bill Shakespeare," says Bruce, placing the large white plate down on the table.

"Excuse me?" Randy asks.

"For your writing friend," explains Bruce, motioning with a

sleeved elbow. "Your memoir writer. William Shakespeare."

"There's only *one* writer here," explains Randy, peeved. "And you're looking at him. *Me.*"

"I … I apologize," says Bruce. "I should have spoken more carefully. Is there anything else I can get you at this time?"

"No," answers Randy, motioning for Bruce to leave. "I have an important letter to finish. And then a chapter in an ongoing book. So … yes. *That'll be all.*"

Bruce bows deeply and retreats.

"Asshole," announces Randy, poking his fork into the mound of pasta. "He was being sarcastic. That was a sarcastic bow. Loser asshole clown with a fucking awful job who has a dream of acting. Never gonna happen because he's a fucking loser clown in a fucking loser awful job. I will pitch a fumy dookie right on his fucking head. I will kick him to the ground and stomp on his spirit. I will subject him to the ground and I will *pound*!"

Lunch has been served.

Felicity, from her attached chair—her large green eyes open wide, her tiny doll mouth just slightly ajar—intently watches the scene taking place in front of her, missing nothing.

It's not difficult to see why Randy pretends to be so attached to her.

This most wonderful lunch goes on for hours.

One can only hope it never, ever ends!

Outsider Perspective!

Lewis Taylor, ACLU attorney: "My name is Lewis Taylor. I'm a lawyer for the ACLU in Washington, D.C. Randy asked me to say a few words about him for his project. I'm still not certain what he wants here. I can tell you about my specific experiences with Randy over the years. Randy's a … vibrant young man. I cannot state that enough. He is a *vibrant* young man. Many and varied headstrong opinions about, let's just say, aspects of life that others might not necessarily devote as much … attention and time to. Randy is—and I say this with an extreme and deeply rooted respect—quite capable of pushing the limits of what an American citizen can get away with in this day and age—while still being protected beneath the tenuous umbrella of this country's constitution. That is all I care to say!"

WORST PLACES RANDY EVER AWOKE AFTER A NIGHT PARTYING HIS ASS OFF

Greyhound bus, en route to Atlantic City

Personal grooming aisle at the Dollar Store

VIP Box at a Truck & Tractor Pull

At the dental school, getting a half-off root canal

Dressing room at Men's Wearhouse

In a vibrating massage chair at The Sharper Image inside
Montgomery Mall, wearing an umbrella hat.

Trump Plaza, Atlantic City, playing the Wheel of Fortune slots

Sandals Resort, Bahamas, strapped into a rented parasail

In a puddle of urine, not his own

Inside a Porta-John in Vegas

At a speed-dating event

Mudpit at the Annapolis Renaissance Faire

In an alley behind the Q-107 Morning Zoo studio, dumpster-diving
for krazy kash

At the bar in the White Flint Cheesecake Factory, clutching
a table pager

Face up in a tanning booth

Chapter Seventeen:
A NEW DAWN!

Randy sits patiently in an office waiting room in downtown Bethesda.

"Still pissed off about the Insuck-Ta-Side. That was a genius, once-in-a-lifetime idea. They definitely stole that idea from me. I don't know how. *Hurtful.* But my Van Halen graphic novel is coming along super. I'm still waiting for permission from Dave Lee Roth's people to turn him into a slow-moving zombie who loves cocaine. He'll move at a *normal* pace. It's *very* funny!

"The flavored sex lube is working out phenomenal. I've been mixing and matching in my kitchen. Kinking out some new flavors for women who dig their lube more sour than sweet. And, for the ethnics, fried and spicy.

"Sadly, my SAFE SIT app was rejected by Apple, which is lame, but I'm going to take it solo. Handing out fliers on the Metro starting next week. Viral campaign. Which is *hot.* Going to make it look like I'm being mugged. I have a black friend who could pull it off. He's a scientist now. Knew him in high school. We played D&D when I wasn't playing alone. I was the dungeon master." Randy laughs. "I made the guy carry all my weapons and armor. Haven't talked in awhile. But *great* Facebook friends!

"Which reminds me, I have to send him a thumb's up. Does that cost money? I hope not. Been sending a shit load of thumb's ups to the Arby's Facebook page."

There is a pep to Randy's step. His face glows. He appears to have catapulted himself into a better "space."

"I'm a gunslinger. I feel transformed. I'm almost *vibrating. Glowing.* I feel that I'm on an upswing. And after today … well, I have a very solid feeling about this. A brand new day for Randy Dandy! Let. It. *Begin!*"

"Randy S._____," announces a secretary. "Mrs. K._____ will see you now."

"Kick it out!" says Randy. He gallantly follows the secretary out of the waiting room and down the plush hallway of the law office. The walls are lined with diplomas, awards and expensively framed antique photos of Bethesda, when the streets were lined with street-cars and when men on their way to work wore seersucker suits and straw fedoras.

Randy, wearing a red Maryland Terps T-shirt and a pair of his favorite casual cut-off khaki long shorts, takes in everything.

The secretary introduces us to yet another secretary. "This way please," the second secretary proclaims, leading Randy into a grand office: mahogany desk, hardwood floors, a bronze lady justice sculpture on a pedestal, holding balance scales in one hand, a sword in the other.

Framed desk photos can be seen of a family: a wife, a husband, two sons and a dog.

An attractive woman, sitting behind the large desk in an Aeron chair, stands and extends her right hand. She appears to be around the same age as Randy. Randy leans forward. They shake hands. *Is there a look of recognition in the lawyer's eyes? Perhaps she's read about Randy and his exploits? Has she somehow heard about this infamous local man and his numerous inventions and his many works of written art? Perhaps she's a fan of the Sports Addicts?*

"Please. Have a seat," the lawyer says.

Randy does so.

"Wow! Comfy," he states. "*Whoof!* Real leather?"

"Not fake," answers the female lawyer. And then to the secretary, "Thank you, Liz."

"I had a hard time finding a parking space," begins Randy.

"Bethesda. It ain't like it used to be."

"No," says the lawyer. "Parking is at a premium. Did you park in our lot? We can validate."

"Down the street," says Randy, annoyed. "Jesus. Wish your office had told me that before. Now we gotta make this under an hour."

"That shouldn't be a problem," answers the lawyer, smiling. She glances at the clock on the wall. "How may I be of assistance to you today? You told Rachel, my paralegal, that you're in dire legal straits?"

"*Ha*! I did," says Randy. "Yeah. That's what I said."

"And? … You're not?"

"Sort of," says Randy. "Kinda, I guess. It's complicated."

The lawyer takes out a yellow legal pad. "Let's start at the beginning. Basic. Name?"

Randy hesitates. "Randy. Randy S._____."

If the lawyer recognizes the name, she does not show it.

"Occupation?"

"Full-time artist."

"Okay. What type of artist?"

"*Life* artist."

The lawyer begins to jot down a notation … but stops. She looks up. "And who is your friend?"

"*This* guy? My memoirist."

"Your what?"

"You don't know what *memoirist* means?"

"Not the way you just pronounced it. Someone is writing your life story?"

"Yes." Randy shrugs. "That's typically what a memoirist does."

Randy laughs. The lawyer does not.

"Anyway," says Randy. "I never learned to type. And your boy ain't about to start now!"

"I'm a defense lawyer. You're aware of that, correct? Are you in any sort of legal trouble? And is this on or off the record?"

"Again, it's complicated," answers Randy.

"Let's cut to the chase," says the lawyer. "Why are you here?"

"You really don't remember me, do you?"

"Am I supposed to?"

"Let's cut the shit, right?"

The female lawyer's eyes narrow. "Okay. Let's cut it."

"Do you remember Mam-Mam?"

"Mam-Mam?" asks the lawyer. "Um, I don't … "

"Of course you do," says Randy. "You used to call her *Slam Jam* as a joke. As if that was funny. But I'm over it."

"Who are you?" asks the lawyer.

"Who *am* I?" Randy says, mysteriously.

"Yes. Who *are* you?"

A grin. "I'm Randy. Randy S._____. And you're Mel. Mel K._____. Formerly Mel T._____. Ring a bell?"

"Oh my god," says Mel, her left eye twitching from excitement.

"Bang bang, baby girl! You're doing okay for yourself! *How the hell ya been?!"* asks Randy, meaning it.

"It's … wow. *Randy.* It's been … far too long."

"Indeed it has," says Randy. "Long time no kiss. I reached out years ago on your Erols.com email account. You never got back."

"I haven't had that account since college."

Randy grins. He knows better. "That's not what your mom told me when I pretended to be your psychiatrist."

"Excuse me?" asks Mel. Now it's her right eye that begins to twitch. "You called my mom? And you told her you were my *psychiatrist?"*

"Years ago. How is she, by the way?"

"She's dead."

"Oof. I'm so sorry," says Randy, but makes a face as if to imply, *Not really. She treated me worse than a bug sucked into an Insuck-Ta-Side.*

"Randy, you told my assistant you needed legal help. Is that not true?" Mel's face is flushed a deep crimson, perhaps as a result of the great excitement from seeing such an old friend after so very long.

"No. I need anything but legal help. I'm doing very well these days, thank you. My town home is worth $1.5 million. That's a lot. And I'm the president of my development. Or used to be, before it was stolen. But that's not why I'm here. So, before I begin, I do want to apologize. And I say that as a thirty-four year old man, even though I have been told many, many times that I look no older than twenty-one. Okay?"

"Okay ... "

"But I think back on that night often. In some ways, it was the best night of my life. In other ways, well, not so much ... I'm sure you feel the same."

"To be honest, I don't know what night you're referring to."

"Mel. *Come* now—by the way, are you married? You have a new last name."

"I am, yes," says Mel, motioning to the framed photo that sits behind her. "We just celebrated our tenth."

"Someone from Churchill?"

"No, we met at law school."

"I've slept with more than forty-six women," states Randy frankly, as if no big deal. "I'm forgetting the exact amount."

"That's ... wonderful."

"Thanks. Back to the night, I was *young*. It was the magic night. The night I made you cry. The night I couldn't pull off the trick. I had zero idea that the rabbit would be dead when I was up on stage! You know, creek rabbits are a lot like homeless—"

"Ah," says Mel. "*That* night. I mean, if I remember, I wasn't crying because of the trick. I was probably crying more because of all the attention that you were calling my way—"

"I knew very little about creek rabbits," Randy interrupts.

"Randy ... it's terrific to see you again. It's been far too long.

I would love to chat about old times ... at a *later* date. I'm extraordinarily busy this morning. I have a very difficult case in Rockville tomorrow, very early. And I'm afraid—"

Randy makes a "shhhhhhhhh" motion.

"You're making us both look bad. Just calm down. I never forgot you, Mel, and I'm pretty sure you never forgot me, even though you might now be pretending as much. I was your first kiss. Am I wrong?"

"I ... yes. I suppose you were. I guess." Mel glances to the clock on the wall. She stands. What could she possibly have to do that's more important?

Randy asks a bit shyly: "May I be so bold as to ask: Was I a good kisser?"

"Randy ... I cannot tell you how long ago this all was for me. It feels like worlds and worlds ago. Honestly. Ages, really ..."

"Can I ask you a personal question? Why did you break up with me? Was it because I couldn't pull off the trick?"

"It had nothing to do with that. No. I mean, it was so long ago."

Mel starts to make her way to the door. Randy also stands, reaches into his *Big Pecker's Bar & Grill* tote bag, and produces a magician's hat.

"A magic hat?" the lawyer asks. "Why—*oh Jesus.*"

"Righto," says Randy, now pulling out a wand. "In my mind, very *little* time has passed." Randy snaps his fingers as if to accentuate the quick passage of time. "Do you ... do you ever think about me? You know, occasionally, sometimes even in moments of passion?"

Randy stands between Mel and the closed office door. Mel looks longingly at the door and makes a motion to it. Randy steps to his left, blocking her.

"No. I—"

"I always meant to ask. How did you lose your virginity? How old were you? I was sixteen. The woman was twenty-three. She was later arrested for robbing an Orange Julius at Montgomery Mall. She now has four kids with five different husbands."

"Randy, I really don't want to talk about personal matters. In fact—"

"ONE!" Randy yells, magic wand waving inches from Mel's face.

"Don't tell me …"

"TWO!"

"Are you out of your fucking mind—"

Randy steps forward and presents the hat to Mel.

"You gotta be kidding me," Mel responds, taken aback. *Is this really happening? After all this time?*

It is.

"*Pull it*!" screams Randy loudly, in his best Great Randoni voice. "PULL IT HARD!"

Mel glances to the door. Where could she possibly want to go with the Great Randoni standing before her?

"PULL IT!" the Great Randoni screams again. *When the Great Randoni orders, there is no refusing.*

And yet, Mel shakes her head no.

Instead, Randy reaches into his own magic hat, back nearly thirty years, into a past that Mel mistakenly may have felt was long over. It isn't.

Now it's Mel's turn to scream.

"My god! It's *alive*!"

"Yes!" says Randy. "That's the *point*! Here take it."

He hands it over.

"You lunatic!" says Mel. "Get the fuck out of my office! *Fucking crazy person*! And take this back!"

Mel's secretary, Liz, now barges in. Her eyes, too, appear to be twitching from all of the excitement. She puts a hand over her mouth. "What in good Christ—"

And now it's her turn to scream. In response, the rabbit, perhaps a bit overwhelmed, urinates.

"Put a hat under that," says Randy, still standing between Mel and the door. "Here. I wrote this for you. It's the latest installment of my Zyngïan chronicles. You're now a *queen*. And you may *keep* that."

He grandly hands over to Mel a thick sheet of papers.

Security arrives.

But Randy is well prepared. He makes a motion as if to say, *I am of no harm! We are old high school lovers, pleasantly reconnecting after many years. She may keep the rabbit, the one that I have successfully pulled out of a hat this time. I did it correctly. Yes, it is very much still alive.*

"That went well," says Randy, a few hours later. "I feel better. A burden has been lifted. I just wish I knew about that parking validation *before*."

The *Potomac Almanac* will soon come knocking but Randy will refuse to open his front door. He has no more time for that.

This is the first day of the rest of his life.

Randy is a man re-born.

But more importantly, there is a party to plan. Perhaps the biggest of Randy's life.

Here comes Randy now!

It's True!!!
Randy's favorite musical is *Barnum*.
His least favorite? *Hamilton*.

MORE OF RANDY'S HATES

Chinese desserts like those cookies with a stupid nut in the middle

People who pronounce "Randy" as "Wandy"

Married women who go by "Miss"

Unmarried women who go by "Mrs."

Those too afraid to call a sparrow a sparrow

Spelling

Soccer

When dogs have tails that go up and he can see their assholes

TV magicians who use special effects

People who throw up in public

Anything that stinks of old

Mr. Pibb

That "feel sorry for me face" that Mel Gibson always makes

Nudity in Holocaust documentaries

Mr. Wendel from the rap group Arrested Development

The ad campaign "Hungry For Clams"

Disrespectful Australians

Chatty Lyft drivers

Ceramic little babies

Anything "beach-wood aged"

Humans who dress as food and hand out fliers

Hair on girls' nips

Driving people to the airport if it's not an emergency

Driving people to the hospital if it's not an emergency

Unfunny banner planes

Stinky candles that smell like girl

Women who have to make an issue out of everything

Bizarre 'gasm sounds

That phrase "it ain't race, it's grace"

Glen Echo Park

Dentists who don't have TVs to watch while getting
your teeth pulled

Chapter Eighteen:
FULL CIRCLE!

"In some ways, it was the best writing I've ever done," says Randy sadly, sitting on the edge of his very large, very round, very king-sized bed.

There is less than one hour until the start of his annual winter holiday party and Randy still hasn't yet dressed. "It's a shame Mel sent all these papers back to me. Just *try* telling me this is no good! I'll crack you to the fucking ribs, chooch!"

Randy recites from memory:

"*Queen Mel sits on her golden throne. The dwarf slave, Giblet, takes a glance up her royal silk skirt. What he sees would blind a normal man, but Giblet is anything but a normal man. Giblet says not a word in his high-pitched midget voice. He takes a bite out of his Bojangle's Biscuit. Fake butter drips down his tiny chin and then on to his tiny, adorable lap. Between Giblet and King Randy, there is an understanding—silent but deadly—that perhaps among the many hundreds who live within this universe called Zyngïa, there are perhaps only two—and these two alone—who have seen Queen Mel's 'fiery gates of Zomoloff.'*"

"I mean, that's good, *right*? 'The fiery gates of Zomoloff.' That means *vagina*. But I have a feeling Mel never even read it. She sent it back. As if I don't have another copy. And that's disappointing. Maybe she's not a reader. A lot of women aren't. She could be one of those who are just into money and politics. Not art. But I'm an adult now and I say this with all honesty: I really do hope we become great Facebook friends. I just sent her a request."

Randy holds up an envelope from a law firm that arrived with today's mail. "But I do wish she hadn't sent me a legal bill for $350.

And I do wish they hadn't sent the rabbit back. Wasn't looking to take care of a new pet. *Not cool, yo.*

"I mean, whatever happened to the friends and family discount?" asks Randy. "That's a lot of money for her to bill me! For the normal person. But I guess I ain't so normal. I'm like the dwarf Giblet. But taller. And with fewer sexual problems. And you know what? I'm *still* going to send Mel my memoir when it's completely finished. *That's what type of guy I am.*"

He tosses the heavy-paper stock envelope with the legal bill into his Washington Redskins themed bedroom trashcan, and lets a freaky one fly.

"Wa-*whooooooo*! Remind me to jot that one down in my Fart Journal. That's a four. A *five* if I'm in a good mood. Which I probably would be after smelling that one. But I can't smell it. I'm too used to it. Occupational hazard. Regardless, *D flat.* I have *perfect* pitch.

"The human body. 'Tis a wonder, ain't it?"

"*Perfect pitch, Randy! Perfect pitch!*" exclaims the Dodger, next to Randy.

"So," continues Randy, petting his pet rabbit of two days, Fugs Funny, "my holiday party is in twenty minutes. You might be thinking, *Hey! Who in this development would ever come to Randy's holiday party?! Especially now that he's no longer the president of the development!* Well guess the shit up? *Everyone's* coming. 100%. Ponder *that.* I got the *touch*!"

Randy strides into his walk-in closet to prepare for his special holiday guests. His cologne collection sits handsomely on a shelf, in alphabetical order, beginning with *Alegria* and ending with *Zippo Silver.*

"Biggest collection in Southern Maryland," announces Randy. "There's an asshole in Hagerstown who has a larger one. But he's an asshole. And he's in *Hagerstown.*"

After much careful and close deliberation for this exceedingly special occasion, Randy chooses *Eternity* by Calvin Klein, shakes out a few drops and slaps it on both cheeks. Randy quickly chooses his outfit for the night, dresses, and heads downstairs.

In the kitchen, Roger Dodger is now standing on his tip-py-toes on the highest step of an eight-foot tall ladder. The Dodger is attempting to hang decorations according to Randy's exacting party standards. The Dodger's concentration is deep.

"To the *right*, Roger," says Randy. "C'mon, man! This is *mucho* important."

Roger, ever the fan of Randy's impeccable taste, adjusts the nude Santa cut-out a smidge to the right. The Santa is receiving oral pleasure from a very attractive female reindeer. The reindeer's anus is a Christmas star.

"And ... *perfect-a-mundo*!" eyes Randy, squinting. "Now careful getting off there, bruv. That's all I need! Another asshole suing me for breaking his goddamn neck!"

As the Dodger weaves a bit on the ladder before unsteadily climbing down, Randy places Fugs back into his wire cage.

The doorbell chimes. It's the 1987 hit song, "Radioactive," by the British rock supergroup the Firm. Tony Tone has just had it installed. And it sounds *terrific*.

Randy strides over to the door and opens it. It's the caterer with all of the delicious food for tonight's event.

"Right this way, kid," announces Randy, leading the delivery-man through the foyer and into the kitchen. "Place all of them yum-mies right there on the counter. *There's a boy.* Nope. Right over there. *There*!"

Randy slices off a few bills from the top of his thick stack and presents it to this most appreciative of deliverymen. "There but for the grace of god go me," says Randy, pointing to the fifty-something man wearing a Lido's Pizza cap.

The deliveryman is at first puzzled but then smiles. Grateful for his $3 tip, he exits quickly. Or tries to. He has a terrible limp.

Within moments, the first guest of the evening arrives. It's Harriet B._____.

Panting next to her is her comfort dog, Benedict.

"Harriet! Benedict!" exclaims Randy. "So nice to see you again! Harriet, you're looking as lovely as always. And Benedict! What a handsome fella!"

"The smell finally came out," says Harriet. "Had to wash him a few times."

"That old age home really stinks!" says Randy, by way of explanation. "But the old people loved him! That was so nice of me to take him there as a comfort dog, yeah!"

"He stunk more like cigarettes and booze," Harriet says.

"Tee hee *hee*!" laughs Randy. "Old timers! They really know how to party! Take a seat, take a seat!"

Leigh C._____ is the next to arrive, along with his beautiful wife, Bets.

"Leigh! And wife! *The great white hope!* To what do I owe this rare and wonderful pleasure?" asks Randy, hugging both.

"We wouldn't miss it for the world," answers Leigh. "*So* excited!"

Bets nods but says nothing. Perhaps she's feeling shy around someone about whom she's heard so much.

"*Welcome!*" says Randy, pointing to the living room. "Plenty of square pizza! Square pizza for the square spook!"

"Not a spook, Randy. *Private* communications," corrects Leigh. "Not government related in the *least*."

"Righto," says Randy. "Not according to these papers I found in your trash! Naughty *naughty*!"

"You found that in my trash?"

"What can I say? I'm the curious type! Hit the living room!" Randy says, already moving on to his next guest, Arnold, who stands before the door. "Bam Bam! *Great to see you*! *Still* waiting for those

Skins tix! I know, I know! Your son wants to bring his friends! But, man, I would *love* to get to that Dallas game next season!"

"I'll see what I can do," answers Bam Bam. "Might have an extra seat, although my sick father should be visiting from West Virginia for that one. He'd love to attend perhaps his last-ever game—"

"Fantastic!" says Randy. "That would be awesome. I haven't been to a Cowboys game in *forever*! This will be fun!"

The rest of the neighborhood association arrives. No one appears to be missing. The turnout is beyond excellent. *What excitement!* Randy was not exaggerating. He seldom needs to. *This is the hottest ticket going!* Before long, the room is bustling with talk and laughter and much frivolity.

The sole exception might be Nora, the new, unpopular president of the development, who sits by herself, a leader alone, shunted both physically and emotionally aside in favor of Randy, who still officially remains the "president of fun." Nora appears to be very lonely. It is a position that Randy wouldn't wish on anyone, except for perhaps Nora.

A tremendously loud car horn can suddenly be heard. The noise of those enjoying the party—rising high and oscillating—comes to a quick and sudden halt. Randy, standing on a kitchen chair before his celebrators, aims his keychain with the bottle opener toward the front door, and the car horn stops. Randy now presses the remote-start system for his 2010 Hummer H3.

"*New car alarm*!" Randy announces. "You might recognize it. 'Fly' by one of my all-time favorite groups, Sugar Ray! Classic song! Perfect for *scrumpin'*! Tony Tone couldn't make it tonight. Some bullshit about his wife giving birth."

It is, indeed, one of Randy's all-time favorite songs. He presses his keychain again and the alarm switches off.

"Not to worry now! This will be *real* quick and then I'll let Nora, the new president, speak! Just want to say a few words and I'll let everyone return to partying their As off!" says Randy. "I want to thank you all for stopping by. I love you all! Or most! *Some*. Here's to a happy and healthy Christmas and New Year's! *Saluth*!"

"*Salud*," says the Australian banker.

"Jesus. Mr. Correcto," says Randy.

"*Doctor* Correcto. I have a PhD."

"La di da. I also have a ThC."

"*D*. And P."

"Fuck you. And the kangaroo you rode in on. Anyway, *salood*!" He shoots the Australian a cutting look. It is more than well deserved.

The party-goers applaud vigorously.

"*It's mid February*," someone says quietly. "*The holidays were weeks ago. Why is this happening?*"

Randy remains standing on the kitchen chair. The applause dies down. Randy glances around.

"No questions?"

The partiers shake their head in unison, as if to say, *No, Randy. We just want to party our As off in your amazing $1.5 million town home! We've missed coming here!*

"Well, I guess I do have one question," says Harriet. "I'd like to know why you're wearing a Navy uniform? Especially if you've never been in the Navy."

"Leave it alone, Harriet," replies a bald-headed young man, standing next to another bald-headed young man, both wearing tight cashmere sweaters and crisp slacks. "Who cares?"

"With a SEAL trident, no less," continues Harriet. "That's … that's *something*."

"As you may or may not be aware," answers Randy patiently, "I very easily could have been a Navy SEAL if I only chose to go that route. Instead, I chose to take care of my Mam-Mam. But I passed the requisite test many times. In my backyard alone. Besides," Randy finishes, "I will have you know that I'm very good Facebook friends with a few Navy SEALS. And I wear this outfit to honor them. And

I happen to look very striking in dress whites."

"My ex would be thrilled to hear about all this," says Harriet. "He's a former Navy lieutenant."

"And I honor his brave and uncompromising duty to our country," declares Randy formally.

"He died. In the first Gulf War."

"So he was the one, huh? Then I honor him even more deeply."

"Let's get on with this," mumbles one of the bald-headed men.

"Where's Mary Mary?" asks Randy, glancing around.

"She suffered a stroke on Tuesday," answers Leigh. "You didn't know?"

"*Shiiiiiiiiiiiiiiit*," declares Randy. "That sucks. And her hot ethnic nurse? The one from the island?"

"Probably working for somebody new," explains Leigh. "Mary Mary's dead."

"Dead?" asks Randy.

"Dead," says Leigh.

"Jesus," says Randy. "Wow. Life, I tell ya. I guess I did notice a slight hitch in her get-a-long. And Roger Dodger? Party can't start without no Roger Dodger!"

The guests, almost in unison, glance around the kitchen and living room. The Dodger is nowhere to be seen.

"Let's just start anyway," says Leigh. "*Please.*"

"Not so fast, kemosashs," says Randy. "The Dodger is an integral part of our development family."

"More like *developmental*," says someone who wishes to remain anonymous and who hired a lawyer to make that wish come true.

Suddenly, Roger the Dodger appears, barreling into the room. "Sorry, Randy! *Sorry, Randy*! I have a *question* for you now!"

Randy looks very surprised. He wasn't expecting this. "I'm *very* surprised! Sure, Roger Dodger! I'm *very* surprised! I wasn't expecting this question. What might the question be?"

Roger's brows furrow in tremendous concentration. "Will you ... will you ever consider becoming the president again? You know? Again? Because we love you so so *so* much!"

"Interesting," answers Randy. "Very ... interesting question. And *well put*. I wasn't expecting that question. I ... I never contemplated as much. But let me just ask: Might there be anything in the bylaws that would preclude me from running again and not waiting another year?"

"No!" Roger yells. He pumps his fists in the air. "*No way!*"

"Oh for god's sake," exclaims Nora from the corner. "Are you fucking kidding me?! You're using this poor kid to do your bidding? I'm the president now. Why are you even up there talking?"

Randy makes a sad face. "I am afraid that Roger might know more about the bylaws than anyone else here, Nora. He's very rarely wrong. And this is my house."

"*Very rarely wrong!*" echoes the Dodger.

"And he's hardly a kid," continues Randy. "He's twenty-three. Or four. Or whatever."

"*Rarely wrong?* He has the IQ of a sweet potato!" screams Nora.

"*Sweet potato!*" says the Dodger.

"Hurtful," says Randy. "That's very hurtful, Nora. I love sweet potatoes. And I love the Dodger. He's sweet. Like a sweet potato."

"This is absurd!" says Nora, not very convincingly.

"*Absurd!*" says the Dodger.

"Look at you," says Randy to Nora. "Like ya *own* the place. So comfy. Big ol' lazy she-cat, lying in the sun. All aboard the Rollercoaster Estrogen. This one's got some real loopy-di-loops. *Real annoying twists and turns. You need to shift out of F and down to M ... for male.*"

"Cut the shit! I'm the president!" says Nora, not very convincingly. "And that's it. *Jesus!*"

"True," replies Randy patiently. "But I propose we take another vote. Just, I don't know. To be *sure* …"

"It wouldn't hurt, Nora," says Bam Bam.

"Yeah, just a quick vote," adds Leigh. "It really wouldn't do any harm."

"Quick vote!" says the Dodger. *"Cut that shit!"*

"Oh, you have to be kidding me! You have got to be *fucking* kidding me! Is he paying you all off? He *has* to be paying you all off!" exclaims Nora loudly.

It is not a good look.

"So let's vote," announces Randy, without the slightest hint of ego. "Who here would like to have Randy as the development's president again? Please raise your hand."

Hands across the room shoot into the air.

"And who here would *not* like Randy to once again become president?" asks Randy.

Nora raises her hand and looks around. The only hand now raised belongs to—not surprisingly—*hers.*

"Unbelievable," she says. "Just incredible. What did it take? *Just tell me.* If anything, just tell me how much it took. I'm *curious.*"

The room is quiet.

"Just fucking tell me!" Nora declares, slightly unhinged.

"Okay!" answers the banker from Australia. "Randy will be paying all of our yearly dues. Okay? That's not chump change, Nora!"

"Chump change!" echoes the Dodger.

"And the mandatory flags!" Nora asks somewhat weakly. "And funny mailboxes? And the half-off gutter crabs that sickened us? You're all okay with all that shit?"

"Gutter!" screams the Dodger. *"Crabs!"*

"Oh, give it a rest," says one of the bald-headed young men. "Who cares, Nora! Just fly the damned flag! And put in a funny mailbox! We're talking $8,500 a year! You have nothing better to spend it on?"

"*Damn flag!*" says the Dodger. "*Spend it on!*"

"The figure is arbitrary! He made up that amount! Under my leadership, it'll be much less!" declares Nora, defensively. "It's just *fantasy*!" She points to Randy. "He lives in his own goddamn world!"

Randy shakes his head. "*Nora.* Nora, my dear. That figure, that specific figure, that figure was reached after much and *careful* consideration."

"So all of you want this moron to be president again?!" asks Nora, appearing more and more desperate. "Really? Another goddamn year with this baby buffoon?"

"I don't wanna dance, Nora. I'm sportin' too huge a pair of sizzlers," Randy says, a bit sadly.

"*Baby buffoon!*" says the Dodger. "*Another year!*"

"I think we're ready," declares Randy, making his now traditional pope motion with two fingers.

Randy points to the Dodger, who presses a red button within a small black box.

"Check *this* out!" announces Randy, grinning widely.

There's a dull *pop*.

A bass-heavy and sparkled explosion reflects both sound and light off the town home's windows.

Fireworks!

"*Fireworks?*" asks Nora. "Are you fucking … and how much did that cost? Dear *Christ*! Is this even legal? And on a Tuesday night? In the middle of February?"

"I'd say it is *more* than legal," declares Randy. "And the price doesn't much matter, does it? *So* cheap. From Mexico. So, actually, no. It's *not* legal. But so awesome. You want to know why? Cause I will do *anything* for my constituents."

"*Not legal!*" says the Dodger. "*Mexico!*"

To the crowd, Randy says eloquently, "I work for *you*!"

"*You!*" screams the Dodger. "*Mexico!*"

The colors are magical, dancing and swirling and twirling for the enjoyment of not only the development's residents, but presumably for most of Montgomery County and perhaps even observers as far south as the mountains of central Virginia. Future generations will talk of these holiday fireworks on a Tuesday night in mid-February in awed and hushed tones.

"Bye," says Nora, making her way out the front door. "Enjoy your new president, assholes!"

She stops before exiting. "And Randy? *Fuck. You!*"

Harriet's comfort dog, Benedict, begins to yowl with what can only be described as pure pleasure from the sounds and sights of the very noisy fireworks still crackling overhead in orgasmic, colorful release.

"I won't include any of that in my memoir, doc," says Randy. "If you apologize. *Immediately.*"

"Not on your life," says Nora.

"I will give you one more chance," Randy says. "Apologize. Or ye shall appear in my book as you thusly appear in thee *actual* life!"

"Not on your life," Nora sputters. "Not. On. Your. *Life!*"

"Looks like we're about to jump on the *S.S. Female.* And we're about to hit *choppy* waters," sighs Randy. A few laugh heartily. "But, Nora, I really would like to offer you a most *precious* gift—and that would be the gift of *forgiveness.*"

"*S.S. Female!*" says the Dodger.

Nora, like a petulant child, does not respond. She exits lamely.

"Well, it *is* getting late," says Bam Bam, checking his phone. "Thank you, Randy. *Fantastic* party!"

"Yeah, Randy. *Amazing* party!" announces Leigh. "Thank you so very much. What *fun!*"

Leigh's wife, still not over her initial shyness, shuffles out without so much as saying a word. Randy sometimes finds that his mere presence can be a tad intimidating to anyone who has actually met him.

"I'll see about those Skins tix for you," says Bam Bam, also making his way to the door. "And I'm *very much* looking forward to this year's 'RandyFest'!"

"That's right!" says Randy. "I forgot all about that! Now a three-day festival! And the petting zoo is gonna happen! With animals borrowed from the National Zoo! Write it down! For this summer! Just waiting to hear back about the Chinese pandas!"

"*RandyFest*!" says the Dodger. "*Pandas*! *Waiting to hear*!"

"Gonna have strippers again?" asks one of the two bald-headed men. "At RandyFest?"

"*Strippers*!" yells the Dodger.

"*Hail* yeah! The hottest strippers in *all* of southern Maryland!" asserts Randy happily. "Dancing to some fresh tuneage from yours truly! Oh man! You will *love* these women!"

"Looking forward to *that*," says one of the bald-headed men. "Sounds like a *lot* of fun!"

"Yes," agrees the other. "*Most* fun indeed."

"And the *edibles* at the bake sale!" says Randy, excitedly. "Mark your calendars! April 20th!"

The bald-headed couple leave together.

The party has been a resounding success.

From within his cage, Fugs Funny, the magical rabbit, joins Benedict in squealing and yowling in pure delight.

"I forgot to mention!" yells Randy, over the pop-pop-*poppin'* of the fireworks, "that everyone who lives within this development will receive 15% off my upcoming memoir! Except for Nora! Who gets it for *free*! Compliments of *me*! When it comes out! Which should be really soon! It's going to be *fucking amazing*! You're going to be hearing about it right here! Book party right *here*! So … thank you again for coming!"

"*Party*!" says the Dodger. "*Coming*!"

After the last guest reluctantly exits, Roger Dodger, who has been manning the front door, closes it. He then pumps his fists above his head much like a heavyweight boxing champion. "*Number one! Number one!* Number *one*! *Randy*! Number *one*!"

"C'mere," says Randy.

The Dodger follows.

"Not you, dummy."

"Ok*ay*-dokie!" says Roger.

"Jesus. Go watch your cartoons."

"I love Randy!"

"*Noah*. Follow me."

Randy grabs a bottle of wine and two Redskins mugs. He walks past Mam-Mam's old rattan chair in the living room, past the empty lizard terrarium filled with unwashed pebbles from the Falls Road public golf course and the plastic, multi-tiered McMansion that Turk Wiggler used to reside within but that has now been decorated and placed in a large wire cage to accommodate its brand-new occupant, Fugs Funny.

"So I wanted to thank you for being here this past year, co-writing this memoir," Randy says, making his way up the stairs. "I realize that you're more interested in doing your own thing, your fiction. And I know that you're still working on that silly book about the kid in Spain or whatever the hell it's about. But let's face it: I'm helping you, right? And I hope another year spent following me and writing about me might help you learn even *more* about writing and creativity. And life. More than you'd ever learn at that useless college with your stupid degree. Noah, we have so many adventures to go through together! Will you stay another year with me?"

Randy waits for a reaction. After it arrives, he nods happily. "Good. Your fiction book can wait. No one's going to read it anyway. But that's okay. Everyone has a dream. Maybe one day you'll achieve it. Then again, maybe you won't. I know the economy ain't great out there. Rougher than a whore's tongue!"

He pauses for the laugh that he's sure to arrive.

After it does, he continues:

"Listen, if you want a co-producer credit on my Ocean City voyeur fuck film, it's all yours, okay? Gonna enter it into the Maryland State Film Fest competition in a few weeks. Have a *great* feeling about this one! So *that's* exciting. And I'm already writing my next porn parody, *True Slit*. You can have a producer credit. Or maybe not producer. What's lower? Anyway … let's fucking *drink*!"

Randy walks up one more flight of stairs and opens the door leading out to the town home's widow's walk, the railed rooftop platform that overlooks Randy's gorgeous development that he built and paid for with his own hands.

Or with Mam-Mam's hands.

And money.

Above, the firecrackers dance and skitter to the delight of a crowd steadily gathering below on Seven Locks Road. Cars have pulled over, including a few police cruisers and fire trucks.

Randy cordially pours a glass of wine.

"From a Virginia winery. The biggest. *Very* elite. The box is misleading. So is the price tag. And that the sponsor is NASCAR. Take *this*. Delicious, *right*? Fruity. Or something. Doesn't matter. Let's raise our Redskins mugs to a new year, how's that, Noah? You like *dat*?"

Randy looks down at the development that he's "bequeefed" to all his good neighbors and friends. It has, indeed, been a most amazing year. Another spectacular year lies ahead. There are *so* many plans.

More than that, Randy has met a certain someone "special."

"Can't wait for you to meet Jade. Cheaper than April. And *nice*. A few days ago she told me, 'I can come over at six and fuck your brains out and then you can have your evening.' That's *considerate*. Also, she's cleaner."

Randy presses his keychain and the Hummer's stereo blasts out 'Love in an Elevator' by Aerosmith.

"I *love* life," Randy says. "I really fucking do. And life loves *me*. Wish Tony Tone was here to hear this. Just got a text that his wife's labor isn't going well. I'll send special flowers that I might just find within the development."

Randy winks. The trident insignia on his uniform reflects the exploding colors above. Randy sets the car alarm on "repeat" for the pleasure of his neighbors and constituents.

"Hired a sixth grader to light these Mexican fireworks. Was born with an extra finger. Margin of error is *wide*. Some might say he was *born* to do this job."

Above, the firecrackers dance and skitter to the delight of a huge crowd steadily gathering below on Seven Locks Road.

"It's a strange feeling to know that this development wouldn't exist without me. I live the life I love and I love the life I live. Or something like that. I'm just getting started. God, I wouldn't want to be anyone else! If I was somebody else, then who in the fuck would be Dandy Randy? No one! And I will *never* stop. *Ever*! *Never ever ever ever ever ever ever!* Never! *I'm just gonna keep going and going and going and going*! *And never stop!* Okay, let's stop this. I'm cold. Have to television."

Randy retreats back into his $1.5 million luxurious town home, deliciously warm and inviting, leaving his guest to stand alone outside on the exposed platform, attempting to take it all in.

There's still so very much to accomplish—for both Randy and your humble chronicler.

Sometimes the words of the English language are futile. Greatness is a construct that can be only built brick by brick, by reflecting back what one sees, motion by motion, day by day, on into infinity.

But the words I have just written and that you have now read—I fear they have missed their mark. Just as the stars above routinely explode with an energy that resounds through generations, it will be Randy's legacy that will echo across time and space.

This great man is just getting started, that much is evident. We greet Randy at the beginning of a wonderful, varied, *sui generis* career. And I intend to be there each and every giant step of the way, trying my best to build up his greatness, brick by brick, word for word, tale by tale.

O Randy ... the world implores that you never stop *bequeefing* your greatness to the rest of us!!!

Go, go, Randy ... and never, ever, *ever* stop!!!!!!!!!!!!!!!!!

Author's Note:

So, it's just before we go to press and Randy wants me to write the following, to his dearest, most loyal readers. I find it only fitting that the book ends with *his* beautiful words and not mine.

Take it away, Randy ...

"Hey! This is Randy! I hope you really loved the book you just read. It didn't come easily but I'm *really* happy with how it turned out. I hope it lasts for generations. If you *did* like the book, as I'm sure you did, I want to let you know that I'm really easy to get in touch with. I *love* it when people get in touch! This is true: a guy once wrote to me by mistake. His friend had a similar email address. Turns out that this dude lives in Iowa and works for a tire-rotation place. He has a birthmark on his forehead in the shape of the Playboy Bunny. Isn't that amazing? Before long, I was telling him how much I love the local tire-rotation place here on the Pike. They serve free coffee and sometimes I'll show up just to talk about the Skins. We became really good Facebook friends and we write each other every holiday, except for the Hebrew ones. If you send me a photo proving that you purchased this book, and that you're a hot-ass Betty, I am *so* much more liable to get back in touch more quickly, or at all. That's just the way life works, folks. So thank you again and if you're in the area, please stop by. I'll probably be drinking a cool one on my town home's front stoop. Don't approach. Just yell from a distance 'Randy?!' That's the code!"

How to Get in Touch with Me on the Online

Website: http://www.RandyIsDaDope.com
Email: Numberonelover453@yahoo.com

BONUS!

MAM-MAM'S WORLD-FAMOUS YUM TUM TUGGERER CHICKEN

7 Chicken Breasts

3 egg yolkes

1/2 c honey

1/2 tsp pepper

1/2 c melted butter

1 Tbl salt

1 tsp Paprika

1/2 cup of "secret spice"
(Old Bay)

Mix everything and then put it on the chicken pieces. Bake until done. Down it with Natty Boh. Point to the sky where Mam-Mam currently resides. Shoot her with your fingers. She'd laugh. Maybe blow a kiss. Tell her Randy sent ya! Ask her if Pop Pop is still an asshole. Just joking. No I'm not.